A Rigged Deck

Leon Michaels

Books by Leon Michaels

The Path Home

From the Mists of Darkness

Task Force Nemesis

Tales From The Bench

The Echelon Factor

The Morbius Expedition

Three Against The Darkness

Random Acts Of Science Fiction

Willem

Today is Yesterday's Tomorrow

"The Denoyelles Family Saga"

The Hanover Throne

The Bellus Project

The Bellus Legacy

The Bellus Myth

The Bellus Solution

The Bellus Prophecy

"The Crane Equation Trilogy"

The Crane Equation: The Early Years

The Crane Equation: Rebuilding a Nation

The Crane Equation: The Crane Legacy

"The Black Ops Series"

Operation Damocles

Operation Dokkaebi

Operation Yofune-Nushi

Operation Kartikeya

The Black Orchid

Acknowledgements

To my Wife for line editing, and for giving me her honest opinion without laughing.

This is a work of Fiction. Any similarities to individuals past or present is unintentional and purely a coincidence. Any similarities to any individual in the future is pure Karma.

This page left blank

A Rigged Deck

Byron Matthew Reynolds was twenty years of age when he rode into Baghdad in the turret of a HUMMWV or Humvee leading a convoy of supply vehicles to the grunts engaged in combat. He was a truck driver by training, but his Company Commander used him to man the M2 Browning Heavy Machinegun in the turret since he was better with the weapon than any of the other men in the unit.

He made it through that little war and went home with a Purple Heart from a piece of a shattered bullet that cut his left cheek. Once home he just went through the daily routine of being a Marine, driving trucks from point A to point B as required and never complained about the hours. Bryon was discharged at the rank of Corporal when his time was up, and he returned home to Wagoner County Oklahoma to begin a new life.

Bryon used his savings and training to start a hot shot delivery service. He was helped in starting his business by the fact he was three-quarters Cherokee which gave him an in as a minority business owner. Bryon started with a used Dodge one-ton flat bed and thirty-foot goose neck trailer making deliveries of anything he could contract for around the state and into surrounding states. Within two years he had a new Dodge one-ton and all the work he could handle.

He considered hiring on a couple of drivers and buying more trucks but then he sat down and took a hard look at the outlay for each driver and vehicle. The additional insurance alone would be a burden that he figured was more than the business could handle plus the payments to Workmen's Compensation was ridicules as far as he was concerned. Bryon did buy a two-ton box-bed and scheduled runs according to what he needed on any specific day.

Bryon worked hard, putting money in the bank and even buying eighty acres where he built a house and a large shop to keep his trucks in for maintenance when he wasn't on the road.

Because of his long hours, Bryon had trouble establishing any real relationships with the women he dated. To the world Bryon Reynolds was no one important. But on a cold, fateful day in November, nineteen years after he rolled into Baghdad, he became one of the most well-known and hated individuals in the country.

Bryon took a contract to haul two rebuilt postal sorting machines from a repair shop in Arlington Texas to the Postal Distribution Center in St. Louis Missouri. The cargo was two crates, eight feet long by four feet wide by four feet tall. He took the box truck because he would have to hold onto them overnight because of the distance of travel.

This was a COD delivery which meant once he had a signature on the shipping documents, he would submit them to the Postal Service for payment and receive his money within thirty days. He had done this before with other government agencies and had no problem being paid this way.

The maintenance receiving dock was only open from eight in the morning to five in the afternoon. Bryon cleared the gate security check and backed into the unloading dock at seven-thirty in the morning. He decided that since he had time, he would walk around the corner to a Quik-Trip for coffee and maybe a breakfast burrito before Receiving opens for business.

Bryon talked to the security guard at the gate for a minute before walking over to the Quik-Trip. The store was very busy, and he had to wait in line to pay for his coffee and a breakfast burrito which would make him return to his truck after eight o'clock.

He was about one hundred yards from the gate when his truck exploded with the shock wave blowing him out into the street onto a passing car, rendering him unconscious.

Thirty-one men and women died within seconds of the explosion with another fifty-seven seriously injured and twenty-nine classified as walking wounded. The security guard was one of those killed.

When Bryon woke in the hospital's Emergency Room, he began asking questions which pointed the police directly at him. Within hours the FBI were able to prove the truck belonged to Bryon, but all the paperwork pertaining to his delivery was ash as was his cell phone with the contact information for the people in Texas. Bryon gave all the information he could remember concerning the people he received the crates from, but he was told later that all they found was a machine shop that had closed its doors nearly six months before due to the owner dying.

His last hope was the notes on his office desk at home but that became hollow hope when Bryon was advised his house had burnt down the day of the explosion. Without any evidence to support his claim, Bryon was placed under arrest for murder.

Two weeks after the explosion, Bryon Reynolds was formally charged for the murders of thirty-one employees of the United States Postal Service. The trial would take place six months later with the U.S. Attorney prosecuting him painting Bryon as a lone wolf. The fact that his home had burned down the day after the bomb had detonated was ignored by everyone involved in the case.

Bryon professed his innocence, but he had been painted into a corner he could not escape from. Whomever had set him up had most likely figured him to die in the blast, but he was still convicted and given a sentence of death.

There was nothing for Bryon to do except to accept his fate because no matter what he said, no matter how loud he shouted it, no one would believe his story of innocence.

You will feel a slight stick

Time passed slowly for Bryon as he awaited the day for his execution. He was first sent to the Federal Penitentiary in Gary, Indiana but after two attempts on his life he was transferred to Leavenworth, Kansas and placed in isolation where he spent his time reading.

He found it interesting that he was also receiving mail from women all over the country with several proposals of marriage. The women ranged from high school drop-outs to PhD's. For the most part from the photos they sent, they were average looking with bodies ranging from what appeared to be anorexic to very obese. But there were a couple that looked as if they should be walking the runway for Victoria's Secret if the photos told the truth.

Bryon's attorney worked every angle to first get a new trial then a pardon to life in prison without luck. He finally asked not to receive visitors since they were either reporters looking for his story to a famous writer wanting to write his story. Bryon accepted his fate with a quiet calm which puzzled those who watched over him. His attitude became one of just passing the day to the next. In his mind, the scar on his face was a warning of tempting fate, and fate had caught up with him.

When the date of his execution came he was asked what he wanted for his last meal. He only asked for the regular meal being served and nothing more than that. His attorney asked if he had any message for his mother which he replied that he had said all he could say, and there was nothing more to be said.

As he lay on the execution gurney with his arms tied down for the chemicals which would remove his life, he was asked if he had any last words. Bryon just looked at the Warden without speaking. Thirty minutes later he was pronounced dead.

Bryon woke up in light green room with the sun shining through a window which took him a minute to realize that had no bars. The bed was comfortable which made the headache he was suffering a bit more endurable. As his eyes adjusted he looked around the room and to him it seemed as if he was in a small motel room instead of a prison hospital.

As his head cleared he wondered if the execution had failed and he was now someplace awaiting the next attempt to end his life. Slowly he sat up in bed and looked around for a place to relieve his bladder. His body was weak and slow to respond to his internal commands to move as he check the two doors on the opposite side of the room.

The first door opened to a closet with clothes hanging in it which he just closed and went to the next one. This was a full bathroom which he made use of. As he washed his hands once he had relieved his bladder he looked in the mirror and another person looked back at him. His scar was gone, and his face was not the one he had worn all his life. Bryon was staring at the face in the mirror when a voice was heard from the doorway.

"Good, you're up. Why don't you shower, then get dressed? The clothes in the dresser and closet should fit. Once dressed we'll talk as you get something to eat."

The man speaking to him was dressed in a very expensive suit. He was clean shaved with grey showing at his temples and he spoke without a distinctive accent.

"Who are you and where am I?" Bryon asked.

"We'll cover that while you eat. When you are ready, there will be someone in the hall to escort you to where we shall talk."

The man just turned away and left before Bryon could ask any more questions. He stripped out of the pajamas he was wearing and noticed that the Marine Eagle, Globe, and Anchor tattoo he had on his right arm was gone. Bryon had no idea what

12

was happening to him, but he was breathing and above ground for the time being.

When he stepped into the hallway he was met by two men also wearing suits. There was no doubt in his mind that both were armed even if their firearms were concealed under their jackets and they both looked like they could handle themselves in a brawl. Neither man spoke as one just stepped off down the hall, leading the way with the other following behind Bryon.

They took Bryon to an elevator which took them up from the fourth floor, opening on to the seventh floor. Down a long hallway till the man in front opened a door and ushered him in. Neither man followed him into the room. The man who had spoken to him in his room was sitting at a table covered with a white tablecloth and had covered dishes placed upon it.

"Come Mister Reynolds, sit. I believe the meal we have for you will please you."

Bryon moved to the empty chair at the table, sat down then uncovered the plates. He had to smile when he found a large omelet on his plate along with bacon and hash browns. Under another cover was biscuits and gravy.

"This looks good mister, but it does not explain what I'm doing here?"

"Mister Reynolds, my name is Thomas Jameson and I'm an attorney by trade. What you are doing here is the people I represent needed a person with your qualifications."

"Qualifications? Hell, Mister Jameson, the only talent I have is as a truck driver and considering I'm here instead of a coffin, you already know the trouble that got me into. So why don't you spell it out what you want from me while I eat."

Bryon poured himself a cup of coffee from the carafe on the table and cut into the omelet with his fork. He dipped the bit of egg and ham into the gravy and tasted it. Once he knew it was to his liking, he poured gravy over the omelet and hash browns, then added a touch of salt and pepper to the mix. As he ate, Jameson gave him the details of how he found himself here.

"Mister Reynolds, what happened at Leavenworth is simple. We bribed several people to make it look like you died at the hands of your executioner. The body of a homeless veteran close to your height and weight now rests in a grave with your name on the marker. His fingerprints and DNA along with photos we were able to obtain have carefully been replaced with yours in the governments records."

Jameson took a sip of coffee as he watched Bryon continue eating.

"By now Mister Reynolds you have noticed your facial features have been modified. This was done while you were out from the drugs given to you at Leavenworth. In case it has not dawned on you, Bryon Reynolds is deceased which means the person sitting in front of me eating no longer exists. If you accept the offer I will make to you, you will have a new name and history."

Bryon washed the food in his mouth down with a long drink of coffee, then refilled his cup.

"Mister Jameson, what you have said is all well and good, but what is this offer you are going to make me?"

"What my employers would like from you is to be a test subject in an experiment that could be hazardous, even fatal."

"So, I trade one executioner for another? What happens if I say no? Will one of your goons in the hall come in and put a bullet in me?"

"No, Mister Reynolds, but the sentence will be carried out, only this time you'll be buried in an unmarked grave."

14

"What happens to me if I survive this experiment?"

"If you accept the assignment, you will be given a new name as I mentioned, a very sizeable check, and a ticket to any place in the world you wish to spend the rest of your life at the completion of the experiment."

"And what is this experiment that prevented my death?"

"I'm sorry, but that is not available to you at this time. But I will say it can be vital to the defense of this country if successful."

"This country tired and convicted me of a crime I did not commit. What makes you think I give a rat's ass about it anymore?"

"Maybe you've turned your back on the country which I cannot blame you for doing considering how the trial went. Yes, I followed the trial closely, and I think your attorney did a poor job of it. But regardless of your feelings in that matter, what you will gain is your freedom and a new life."

Bryon did not speak as he continued eating until he had his fill. He took one last long drink of coffee before asking the next question.

"When do I have to decide whether I wish to take the assignment?"

Jameson checked his wrist watch before replying.

"Mister Reynolds, you have roughly sixty-seven minutes before the drug that was in your coffee takes effect and fulfills your sentence."

Bryon looked at the coffee cup and shook his head.

"Well I was warned, wasn't I? Now let me guess, if at any time I change my mind, something will be slipped into my cup or glass to finish me off. And if I try to escape those goons will take care of the sentence. No matter what, I am a captive of my desire to stay alive. Alright Mister Jameson, I'll take the job."

Jameson got up from the table and walked to the door, opened it and spoke to the men outside. One of the men handed him what looked a miniature flask. Jameson returned to the table and sat the flask on the table next to Bryon.

"Drink all of what is in this flask. I have been told it tastes like shit, but it will neutralize the poison in your system. But I must warn you there will be no next time. If you fail to meet your end of the bargain, there will be no antidote for whatever kills you. Understand?"

Bryon just nodded as he opened the cap to the flask. He sniffed if and made a sour face, then turned it up, swallowing the contents, trying not to let any lay on his tongue. When he sat the flask on the table he reached for his coffee cup, then paused before picking up the glass of water on the table and drinking the entire glass before speaking again.

"I've tasted some nasty shit while in the Corps and driving trucks, but that beats them all. So, what's next?"

Jameson reached to his right and uncovered a small plate. On the plate was a wallet which he handed over the table to Bryon. Bryon looked at it noticing it was worn. Opening he first noticed a Colorado Driver's License in the name of Bryon J. Petersen.

"Bryon, we figured it would be easier for you to only have to remember a new last name instead of a complete new name."

"Yeah, that it would. I notice the photo is of my new face, how did that happen?"

"We took you photo after the bandages came off, then a bit of creative computer work opened your eyes for the camera. We tried to make as few changes as possible, but you have a new Social Security Number to memorize."

"I guess that can wait until we find out if the experiment works or kills me."

"Bryon, you have at least thirty days before you enter the experiment. But as I said, that can all be explained later."

As Bryon examined the contents of the wallet he was first puzzled by a photo of a moderately attractive brunette that had "With all my love, Rhonda" on the back of it.

"Mister Jameson, who is this Rhonda that I have a photo of?"

"That's your wife."

"Excuse me? Wife?"

"Yes, that too will be explained. And before you ask, that American Express card is real and active. It has a fifty-thousand-dollar limit to it. Use it wisely."

"If I'm still basically a prisoner, why do I need a credit card and what, a thousand in cash in this wallet. Wait, I know, it'll be explained to me."

Jameson laughed then tossed over a room key card.

"This is for your new room. By now all the things that were in the room you woke up in has been moved. Now I must be in LA this afternoon, so I must leave. Mister Petersen, most likely we shall never meet again, so I wish you luck in this endeavor."

Jameson stood and offered his hand to Bryon then left the room. Bryon still had a nasty taste in his mouth but looking at the things on the table he was afraid to touch any of it because he might take another dose of poison and not recover from it. He figured he would go to his new room and see what he might find to help remove the taste from the antidote.

As he walked to the door he put the wallet in his back pocket keeping the key card in his left hand. When he opened the

17

door to the hall, he received the first of two surprises. No one was in the hallway to insure he went to the room which was four doors down from this one.

Bryon walked down to his room, inserted the key card and had his second surprise when he stepped into the room. The surprise was not that the room was a suite, but the fact that there was a woman sitting at the table across the room. A woman whose photo was in his wallet. She spoke first.

"Come on in Bryon. It is a pleasure to finally meet you."

"I'm almost afraid to ask what you are doing here. Is your name really Rhonda?"

"As a matter of fact, it is. My full name is Rhonda Marie Petersen. It was decided to use my last name, so our sponsors only had to construct one set of identification and Social Security numbers. Please come and sit. I have fresh coffee, orange juice and a few pastries here. I have been led to believe the antidote you took tastes horrible."

"Horrible would be a polite term Rhonda."

Bryon walked over and sat at the table and pushed his empty coffee cup to her. As she filled his cup he took a good look at her. She was wearing very little if any makeup and had freckles across her cheekbones and nose. Rhonda was better looking in person, but she would never win a beauty contest. She pushed his cup back over to him and smiled.

"Bryon let me begin by advising you that I work for the people who have need of your services. I am a trained and licensed Clinical Psychologist and my function is to insure you are mentally ready for the task ahead."

Bryon had been sipping on the hot coffee as she spoke. He sat the cup down and looked at her as he spoke.

"What is this task I have agreed to do?"

18

"Bryon, you will be put to sleep, place in hibernation for five years to determine viability of the systems that have been developed for space flight and the possibility of even placing soldiers into such to be thawed out if the term is correct at a later date. Chimpanzees and orangutans have been placed in these same conditions successfully over the past ten years, but we have yet to put a human into the process to insure it is possible."

"Why me?"

"There are several reasons. One is that there are people that believe in your innocence."

"Are you one of those?"

"Bryon, it does not matter what I believe. I'm sitting in this room with you and do not fear for my life. But your attitude during your stay in prison leading up to your execution is interesting."

"Interesting? How so?"

"You must have refused to do a dozen interviews with journalists and turned down an offer to write your story, to let people see your side."

"Rhonda, I could have yelled my story from the top of the Empire State Building and no one would listen. I just figured the only people who would profit from my story was the person writing it and the odds were, they would write it the way they wanted to and not how it really happened. So, I just stayed away from all of them."

"I think I understand. Do you have any questions for me?"

"Only about a hundred, but first, where am I?"

"Officially you are at Milliway's Spa and Resort just outside Reno. In certain circles, Milliway's is also a Rehab Center for the Hollywood elite. One other aspect of this location is they have some of the best plastic surgeons on the planet to take care of celebrities needing work down without it becoming public."

"I take it the work on my face was done here then. How long have I been here?"

"Five months. They kept you in a coma until two days ago and slowly brought you out of it. The bandages came off your face last week."

"So, Rhonda Petersen, what's next?"

"Bryon, you can go anywhere you wish as long as you do not go home. That won't do anyone any good. But when I receive the call that they are ready for you, no argument, we go."

"We go? Then you are my keeper until I enter the experiment?"

"If you wish to look at it that way, yes. Where you go I go."

They talked for a while as Bryon came to terms with his situation he woke up too. The foul taste lingered in his mouth from the antidote, and his throat was a bit sore which was explained by the tube that had been down his throat to feed him.

Bryon told Rhonda he wanted to take a walk, by himself if that was permissible since he had been confined for over five years. She gave him a cell phone and showed him how to use it since it was a much newer model than he had last used. The only number in it was her number and she told him they would meet for lunch at the hotel's restaurant at noon.

As he walked around the broad lawns of the resort he looked from time to time to see if he was being followed but if he was, the individuals were very good at not being spotted. Bryon found an isolated park bench and just sat with the early spring sun in his face and thought about the past years.

He sat and thought about how he had just accepted his fate the first day of Marine Boot Camp and resigned himself to his fate when they drove into Iraq. That feeling had never left him even though he worked hard at making a go of his business. And once he realized that the cards were stacked against him during his trial, he just gave up. No matter what he had said fell on deaf ears.

Bryon thought about what people had gone through to get him out of prison and into whatever project they needed him for. Had fate once again taken charge of his life, or did he have anything he could do about it? He had made a deal to stay alive, even for a short time, but as he sat with the sun on his face, he swore that if he survived the experiment, he was going to find out who had set him up for that bomb.

While in prison, two other bombs had destroyed government buildings, but in those cases, the drivers died. If he had stayed with his truck, he also would have died. Bryon decided there was nothing to do for now except ride this situation out since he had given his word and he would keep it.

His cell phone beeped, and he saw he had a message from Rhonda. She told him she would meet him in the restaurant in ten minutes. Ten minutes meant that he had sat for over three hours thinking about his life and what needed to be done with what was left with it. He had been given a second chance, and he had no intention of screwing it up.

Bryon entered the restaurant via the south patio doors and found Rhonda sitting at a table along the glass west wall. He took the chair opposite her and just waited for the next move. She made it when she pushed a small box over to him. When he opened it, he found a Breitling Chronomat 44 wrist watch. He looked up at her to see her smiling at him.

"Go ahead, put it on." She told him.

"Rhonda, I know I'm a country hick from Oklahoma, but Breitling watches are far from cheap. How much did this set you back?"

"Not a dime. Like you I have a credit card but with a larger amount to use as I want. Our cards are for expenses until we have to part company. No restrictions have been placed on them, and since I knew you did not have a watch, I remedied the situation."

"Thank you." He replied.

Bryon put the watch on and she reached her hand out for the box. He handed it to her and she put it in her large bag then motioned for a waiter. The waiter brought them menus then stepped back as they looked at the list of food.

"Bryon dear, remember what the doctor said about over eating after your illness."

Bryon caught the meaning of her statement. He had not finished the omelet this morning and in the past, he could have cleaned his plate.

"Honey, why don't you order for me? You know how I am about thinking big."

Rhonda order them seafood salads with iced tea. Once the waiter left, she made a suggestion.

"Bryon, after lunch, what do you say about going into town and buying you some clothes more suited to you than what you have already?"

"I take it we have transportation?"

"Of course."

Conversion was polite without referencing the situation Bryon was in, but when they left for Reno with Bryon driving, he opened the topic of her being his make-believe wife.

"Rhonda, the wedding band you are wearing is not new from the indent of your ring finger. What does your husband have to say about your assignment?"

She turned the ring on her finger several times before she answered.

"Bryon, I am a widow. He was in Afghanistan serving with the Special Forces"

"Rhonda, I'm sorry. You have my condolences."

"Thank you, Bryon, but it has been almost five years now. Can we change the subject?"

Bryon asked what was going to happen to all the clothing and such he might buy once he enters the experiment. Rhonda told him a special locker would be in the same chamber he would be in which would hold all his property in storage, so it would be available once he was revived. Neither mentioned the possibility of him not surviving the experiment.

Shopping for clothes was a new experience for Bryon having a woman help him pick out clothing and such. Rhonda would have him try on clothing, looking for that special look a woman would want in her man. Bryon went along with it all and even admitted to himself she had a good eye on what improved his appearance. He did buy a pair of Tony Lama cowboy boots in black which he could wear with anything she recommended.

He did confuse her when he turned into a military surplus store. Bryon told her he wanted things for hiking and maybe hunting once he was out, and if someone else was paying the bill, why not buy those things now. He bought three sets of Marine Green digitals along with two pairs of boots. A field pack along with other items used in back packing including a week's supply of dehydrated foods which had a shelf life beyond the estimated date of his revival.

Several hunting knives, a hatchet and a machete went into the pack along with a six-hundred-foot roll of 550 parachute cord. Rhonda was amazed as he packed the things into the field pack as they were being rang up at the register, and he fitted everything into the pack except the sleeping bag which was attached to the outside.

Back at the hotel he left the field pack in the trunk of their car while taking everything else to the room. As he started to put his things away he was caught off guard by the fact the dresser had her clothing in it as did the closet. Rhonda was taking tags and labels off his things as he was putting them up.

"Rhonda, where are you staying? I mean, what room are you in?"

Rhonda stopped what she was doing and slightly blushed as she answered.

"Bryon, we are supposed to be married so I'm sleeping in this room too."

"Rhonda, but there is only one bed."

"Oh. Don't worry, I'll sleep on the couch, so I won't be a bother to you."

"No Rhonda, I'll sleep on the couch. My mother would skin me alive if she knew I was sleeping in a bed while a female was on my couch, instead of the other way around. No, you will have the bed. End of discussion."

"Alright Bryon, but I'm okay with the couch. Thank you."

Dinner and the conversation between them after dinner back in the room was casual, but Bryon understood Rhonda was slowly working in his head to see how he was dealing with the situation he had found himself in. He kept the answers to any questions as honest as he felt he needed to pass this psychiatric exam prior to him entering the experiment.

24

It had been a long first day for him and when he began to yawn, Rhonda cut off the questions and went into the bedroom to return with the things needed to make out the couch for sleeping. She suggested he change and do what he needed to do, then they would turn in for the night.

Bryon rarely wore anything to bed except his boxers, but sharing a room with Rhonda, he put on one of the sets of pajamas supplied and upon returning to the sitting room found she had made out the couch for him.

Rhonda went into the bedroom and closed the door behind her. Bryon turned out the lights and just sat on the couch once more pondering what was happening and his place in it. He lost track of time until the bedroom door opened with Rhonda back lighted by a light from the beds night stand wearing a cotton nightgown that hid everything.

"Bryon, I'm going to leave the door open, not as an invitation, but because if the night brings anything to you I need to hear it."

"Anything such as a nightmare brought on by PTSD?"

"Yes. Between Iraq, the bombing and trial, then the time in prison concluding with your execution should traumatize anyone. Please understand I am here to help you if I can."

"I understand Rhonda. Good night."

"Good night Bryon."

He watched her walk to the bed, turn off the light, then get under the covers lighted by the moonlight coming through the bedroom window. Bryon laid down on the couch and realized it had been years since he had slept with a woman and even now did not feel the desire. He was as confused by this situation as he was with everything else happening to him.

Sleep came slowly for Bryon as his mind was occupied with his new situation. He was trapped in his desire to stay alive now that he was free of the death sentence, but was he? This new situation basically put him right back on death row, but without the bars. In prison he had given up, resigned to his fate, but now he had a fighting chance to live. One he had to grasp and hang on too even when he entered the experiment.

Pueblo, Colorado

It had been four days and three nights since Bryon awoke to a new life. Except for politeness and for the publics observation, Bryon had barely laid a hand on Rhonda, and she had made no advances towards him. The conversations between them had slacked off with mostly what to do during the day or what to eat at a specific meal. Bryon figured she had exhausted whatever check list she was working from concerning his mental health and was now just waiting and watching him.

It was during lunch on the fourth day that she finally broached a subject that neither had brought up before.

"Bryon, if you'd like some female company, I'm sure that can be arranged."

"Excuse me Rhonda?"

"It's just that you have been celibate for a long time. I understand our employers can arrange for a female for you to enjoy for a night if you wish."

"No. And this will be the last conversation concerning the subject. I've never been one for one-night stands and certainly not where a paid piece of ass is concerned."

Rhonda was amazed that for a man with his background, the women he had known in his life, he was not eager to just enjoy a woman for a night unlike most men who had been in prison. Then there was his use of the word ass. All during their conversations, he had not used a vulgarity, was always polite when talking to her or anyone that he had spoken too in her presence.

Just as lunch was being finished, he opened a new subject.

"Rhonda, the address on my driver's license says Pueblo, Colorado. Is that a real address, or one made up for the license?"

"It's very real Bryon. In fact, the key to the front door is on our cars keyring. Why?"

"Since there are no restrictions on my movements, and we have a place to go away from here, I think we will go see what Colorado has to offer us. Besides, this hotel is beginning to bother me. Too many self-indulgent people more concerned about appearances than the world outside."

"Alright Bryon. When do we leave?"

"Tomorrow morning after breakfast."

"Okay. I do have to inform our sponsors we are leaving here and where we are going."

"No problem Rhonda. I think I'd like a banana split for dessert. What do you think?"

After lunch, they started packing for the trip. Bryon realized he did not have enough luggage for even the few things he bought, so he went down to the mini-mall in the hotel and picked up a medium sized duffle bag and a couple of other items. Only the bags they would need in the morning were left in the room as Bryon packed the car just before dinner.

At dinner, he slid a small box over to Rhonda. When she opened it, she found a pair of diamond ear studs inside.

"Bryon, I know it was not your money, but you really didn't have to do this?"

"No, but you also did not have to buy me this watch either. So, you can consider the ear studs my way of saying thank you for your companionship these past few days. Besides, can't a husband by his wife something nice from time to time?"

Rhonda had to laugh at the husband joke.

"Certain he can Bryon. Thank you very much."

She took out the pearl studs she was wearing and replaced them with the diamonds. The rest of dinner was pleasant, and they thought about catching a movie tonight, but neither found anything interesting at the theaters and television was even worse.

They ate early the next morning, so they could get as much road time as possible. Bryon pushed hard to put as many miles in knowing they would have to spend one night on the road. They took a motel room at Grand Junction Colorado for the night and asked for twin beds. When the motel clerk looked at them oddly, Rhonda explained she had just had surgery and since Bryon tended to roll around in bed a lot, it was safer for her to sleep separately from him until she was completely healed.

It was early in the evening when they found the house located just off Colorado State Highway 78 a few miles Southwest of Pueblo. It sat back from the highway on an unknown plot of ground, but the nearest house was over a mile away based upon the lights seen in the distance.

Rhonda had Bryon take the master bedroom while she took a guest room that had a full bath, so they would not have to be concerned about sharing in their situation. She found a note taped to the fridge telling them the pantry was stocked with staples and there was a selection of meats in the freezer along with vegetables and luncheon meats in the fridge. They had stopped at an Arby's in Pueblo before coming out to the house so neither were hungry. They just spent the rest of the evening putting their clothes away before showering and going to bed.

The smell of bacon cooking woke Rhonda. She dressed and found Bryon in the kitchen scrambling eggs for breakfast. Rhonda just poured herself a cup of coffee and stayed out of his way. He served up a helping to her then himself and sat down. Neither spoke for several minutes until Bryon broke the silence.

"I'm going into town later to do some shopping. You can stay here or go with me, but I will be back."

29

"I know you'll be back Bryon. No, go by yourself. You have a cell phone and I can contact you if I need too."

They both knew this was a trust issue, one he could not avoid and had to fulfill otherwise he would turn around one day to find a gun pointed at his head. Rhonda never asked what he was going shopping for, and he decided that was something best left quiet until he knew he could get what he wanted.

Bryon made several stops at gun stores and places that sold ammunition. He bought Marlin 1894 lever action rifle in .45 Colt with his new identification and credit card. Both flew through the required background checks, then he went to another store and bought a Ruger Vaquero also in .45 Colt with a five and a half-inch barrel. At the next store, he bought another Vaquero in the same caliber in the shorter four point-six-two-inch barrel. Both pistols were blued in color.

By the time he had finished stopping at stores he had acquired five hundred rounds of ammunition for these weapons. Bryon also bought a pistol belt with ammunition loops and a holster for the belt then a shoulder holster for the other pistol. At a tool outlet, he bought jeweler files and honing stones along with a set of gun smith screw drivers.

When he returned to the house just after noon, he carried everything except for the ammunition into the kitchen and began to tear down the weapons, checking for any parts needing deburred or polished. Rhonda never said a word to him about the weapons as she sat across the table from him, watching as he carefully removed one part after another, then inspected them before reassembly.

He finally broke the silence.

"Rhonda, I'm not sure how in depth your file on me is but when I first got out of the Corps, I did some Cowboy Action shooting on weekends until my work load became where I did not have the time. If I survive this, I'm going to give it a go again. So, relax, if I was going to do harm to myself, there is no need to do the work on these pieces that I am doing."

"Actually, I was wondering what our sponsors were going to say when they get the bills."

"Mister Jameson said there were no strings attached to the money and I wanted to see how clean my new identification really was. I passed the FBI's Insta-Check, so now all I have to do is survive the experiment, then I can start a new life."

Later that afternoon, Rhonda stood behind Bryon as he test fired each firearm, then later watched him clean them before putting them in his closet.

The days were spent reading or going into Pueblo to window shop and maybe catch a movie. Time was beginning to wear on Rhonda, and Bryon was doing everything he could to ease her wait. She commented that he seemed completely calm about the wait and he reminded her that he had just spent five years waiting for his execution date.

Two weeks after arriving at the Pueblo house, Bryon was in bed when Rhonda entered the master bedroom wearing a dressing gown. She stood beside his bed and removed it revealing that she was nude.

"Bryon, I've only taken two lovers since I lost my husband, and the last one was over a year ago. I was not hired to provide you with a sexual partner so I'm not standing here for you, but for myself. If you'll have me, take me as you desire."

"No Rhonda, give yourself as you desire. I'll try to give you what you want, I can't promise you more than that."

Bryon moved the covers back, inviting her to his bed.

Deep Freeze

For the next three weeks Bryon was glad that Rhonda had opened the door to sleeping with him. His own suppressed desires flowed from him, and in one aspect made the waiting much more pleasurable.

Bryon had asked her the second night she was in his bed what her feelings were towards sleeping with him. She was honest in that she had come to like him as a person but doubted there could be any love between them because love requires a future and his future was still to be determined.

Rhonda admitted that in a clinical environment, this would never happen, but the closeness of their situation and his manners in dealing with her brought her own desires to the surface. She never denied him during the day nor did he deny her as they waited for the call for them to leave for the experiment.

Rhonda would often reenter the patient therapist stage of their conversations after enjoying each other and found his upbringing to be one of respect for another. He often voiced his concern for his mother's welfare now that he was gone, but Rhonda was able to explain that to ease his own mind, their sponsors had taken steps to insure she was being taken care of but would not elaborate on how this was being done.

She filed her final report to her employers telling them Bryon was mentally prepared and ready when they were. Two days later she received the phone call that changed both of their lives. Bryon was to report for his part of the experiment.

They loaded the car and had to repack it twice since Bryon had increased his personal items while in Pueblo before leaving. They drove north to the small town of Bushnell, Nebraska in the Southwest corner of the state where they were met by two gentlemen who Rhonda referred to as Doctor's.

From there they were guided West into Wyoming until they turned off Interstate 80 onto what appeared to be a country road then another turn onto a private road. Out in the middle of thousands of acres of wheat fields was a fenced in area with a sign proclaiming this to be a Department of Agriculture Research Site. The reality was that the buildings seen above ground were camouflage covering a former Minuteman missile site.

Bryon was shown a small room to be his quarters until the actual experiment. He was told to change into the clothing provided in the room and place his things in a bag provided. Once he had changed he then observed his property being placed in what almost appeared to be a vault inside another larger room with a capsule in the middle of the room with tubes and wires running to it. He was given two keys to the vault door on a dog tag chain and told he would wear them during the experiment and that those were the only keys to his property.

He had noticed whispered conversations between Rhonda and the personal that were dealing with him, especially one older Doctor who wore a name tag with the name of Browning on it. He received a complete physical and when he returned to his sparse quarters, Rhonda was there waiting for him. She had told the head of the experiment that for Bryon's mental health, they should continue with their relationship until the day of his stepping into the void of the experiment.

For the next three days Bryon was subjected to various exams and tests insuring he was ready for the experiment. Twenty-four hours prior to the commencement of the experiment, he went through a thorough bowel cleansing. Rhonda made love to him one last time the night before and was with him as he processed through the final steps of his pre-commencement checklist.

He bathed in a sterilization shower then only wearing slippers moved into the chamber. He could smell a strong disinfectant odor inside the chamber and everyone present were wearing bio-suits to prevent contamination. Rhonda was there also adorned as the others. Once he was laid out into the capsule, she moved to him, took his hand and wished him luck. Bryon could see a tear on her cheek through the plastic face shield of her mask.

As technicians hooked him into the capsule with IV's in both arms and a catheter for urine removal, Doctor Browning quietly asked Rhonda how she felt about Bryon.

She told Browning that she did love Bryon, but not in the way she loved her late husband. She loved him as a dear friend, one she may never see again, but she was thankful for having known him. What she had not told Browning was that she had told Bryon the night before that unless some man came along and swept her off her feet while he was out during the experiment, she would be there when they woke him up in five years.

Once the capsule was sealed Bryon felt the odd sensation of floating as a coolness swept over his body. His last thoughts were that he would succeed in this experiment and that he would see Rhonda again and try to make a go of a relationship with her if she would still have him. Darkness over took the vision of Rhonda lying naked on his bed waiting for him.

Rhonda stood watching as the high-density glass of the capsule seemed to frost over, obscuring her view of Bryon lying in it. Yes, she had fallen in love with him, as she had fallen in love with her deceased husband. Neither man were alike or had much in common except for her. In many ways, she considered Bryon more of a gentleman, but buried deep inside of him, he had a strength which she hoped would get him through this experiment.

She left the test site for the University of Nebraska where she would teach until time to return to Bryon's awakening. She left with a secret no one knew about her relationship with Bryon, one she felt she needed to hide for the time being.

Forty-One Months Later??

Bryon slowly woke to dim light in trying to peel his eyelids back and a throbbing in his head. His throat felt like the Iraqi desert from breathing the dried, purified air inside the capsule. He sensed more than observed the capsule top being removed as he could only lay still, thinking he had made the journey and survived.

"Bryon, can you hear me?" A muffled voice spoke from his right.

Bryon tried to speak but could not voice an answer.

"That's alright Bryon, we'll get you something to drink in a minute but just lie still as we get you all disconnected."

Lying still was easy for Bryon as he felt as weak as a baby. Removing the IV's was no problem, but the removal of the catheter was almost painful since it had been in so long. All the wires connected to sensors placed on his body were disconnected then a cool, damp rag was placed over his eyes. He felt a straw touch his lips and opened his mouth enough to accept it, and then sucked on it the best he could. The water was cool and tasted a bit metallic as it soothed the dryness in his throat.

"Bryon, we are going to put some clinical shorts on you then set you up. Do not try to help us, just let it happen." The voice spoke again.

The damp rag over his eyes seemed to help as did the cool water eased the dryness of his throat. He had no idea how many people were in the room helping him and at that moment he did not care. He passed the test and all he wanted now was out of it.

Soon they had the shorts on him, then sitting upright with his legs off the capsule base. One person was holding him up from behind then two sets of hands lifted him off the base and into what he figured was a wheelchair. Straps were placed over his chest to hold him upright then someone removed the rag and began to carefully wipe his eyelids with a soft, damp cloth.

"Bryon try to open your eyes, but do not be alarmed if you have trouble focusing at first."

Bryon carefully opened his eyes, blinking rapidly as the dim light bothered them. The optic nerves had not been used in so long they were slow to react and adjust to the light. Slowly the blurs before him became figures then he was finally able to see the doctor standing in from of him in scrubs and wearing a surgical mask.

"Bryon, how do you feel?"

"Weak. I take it the experiment is a success?" Bryon's voice was weak as he spoke.

"Yes and no. Bryon, you were out for forty-one months, eight days. Events are taking place in this country requiring us to revive you early. I don't have time to explain right now, but let me have your keys, we are moving you as quickly as possible to another location."

Bryon tried to take the chain from around his neck but did not have the strength. The doctor reached over and assisted him then handed the keys to another person. Bryon was taken to the same room he had stayed in before going down and after his clothing bag was brought to him and they dressed him.

He caught a view of himself in a mirror seeing the long beard and heavy mustache plus long hair shot with grey at the temples. He was given wrap around dark glasses before they took him to the elevator to the building above them. From there he was put in a large SUV along with all his belongings.

The doctor told him to trust the people that were taking him away from the complex, and if fate was generous, he would see him again soon. They drove south into Colorado then west on a dirt road till they came to a farm house out in the middle of the prairie. He was met there by an older couple who took him to a room in the farm house while the men who brought him carried his things in for him. Soon he was alone with the couple and still had no idea what was happening.

The lady of the house came to him and told him her name was Adelle Montrose and that she was a medical doctor, and her husband Thomas was an Engineer. She took his vital signs and helped him stand as he was weighted. When she put him in an arm chair, he asked her what was happening that required him to be taken out of the research center.

"Bryon, the country is at war right here in the United States. Nukes have been set off in DC, New York City, and Boston on the East Coast. Los Angeles, San Francisco, and Seattle on the West Coast. Government offices all over the country have been truck bombed or bombed with people wearing suicide vests. The country is coming apart as a group of what is best described as Socialists have taken control of the country."

"What happened with our military?"

"The Pentagon was hit as was the White House and the Capital Building. The Vice-President, three Senators and four Congressmen were all that survived because they were all out of the city at the time of the bombings. From what little reports we have received, it seems they are supporting the Socialists."

"The military has suffered massive desertions. What's left have holed up on bases, and they are treating this as a civil war between political factions and have so far stayed out of the fighting other than protecting those government offices that are still in operation. Doctor Browning had to move you because the Socialists are raiding every government research center searching

37

for projects they feel is against their beliefs, or they can profit from."

"How much at risk is Browning in? I mean if they find the underground complex, how dangerous will that be for him?"

"Oh, they will find it, but it will be useless for them. Right about now it is being flooded to prevent anyone from utilizing it. Bryon, according to your records you are thirty-seven pounds, thirteen ounces below the weight you entered the experiment with. We need to get you back up to weight and strong again."

"Adelle, do you know Rhonda Petersen?"

"No, but Doctor Browning told me about her. I have no idea where she is if that is what you are wondering. If Browning makes it here, you can ask him if he knows. Now I'm going to fix you some soup to start the rebuilding process and to allow your stomach to adjust to real food again."

"If it's still there, in that grey bag should be a cell phone. Could you get it please?"

"Bryon, communications are risky even if you can connect with a tower way out here. Who do you want to contact?"

"I just want to know Rhonda is safe."

"Bryon, I understand for you it was only yesterday that you last saw her, but it has been nearly four years for her."

"Doctor Montrose, I am well aware of the passage of time, I'm just concerned considering the situation in this country right now."

"Bryon right now you need to concern yourself with regaining your strength and weight. Now as far as the phones are concerned, the anarchists are monitoring communications. If you are able to connect with her, and one of you says the wrong word, then she is in danger of arrest as you are if they can locate you."

Bryon sat thinking about what Adelle told him as she left to make him the soup she promised. There were too many questions he wanted answers too but felt that his hosts may not supply them. He was not sure he could believe this country had gone as deep into depths of despair as described. Was this part of a test to determine the after effects of the program?

Adelle's husband Thomas came in to Bryon's room later and helped him to the bathroom. As Bryon sat on the toilet to let his bowels remove what little fluids he had to remove, Tom updated the information about the country that Adelle had not disclosed.

Within hours of the destruction of Washington, field commanders took it upon themselves to retaliate against those that broadcast their claims of either sponsoring the attacks or having direct influence on them. North Korea was hit hard with nuclear weapons then invaded by South Korea with support of the Japanese. China announced they were staying out of the war on the peninsula.

Tehran, Iran was leveled, and war had broken out in the Middle East with Israel holding on by their fingernails. Europe itself was in turmoil as Muslims who had immigrated turned against their hosts.

When the fleets stopped their attacks, they returned to the United States, collecting Navy and Marine personal from posts all over the world. The Air Force also returned destroying anything they could not fly off the bases in Europe and Asia except for Japan and Korea.

The Vice President who was from California became President according to the Constitution along with the Senior Senator, also from California. Elections were held six months after the event with liberals winning nearly every seat vacant by the bombings. There were people who claimed the elections were rigged.

It was also during those months prior to the election that radical groups began rioting and committing terror amongst the voters. Once the people were sworn into their offices in Congress, they began to dismantle the military until they were at nearly ten percent of their strength prior to the bombings. The state National Guard units began to also reduce their strength as personal just stopped attending their monthly meetings.

Guerilla units composed of prior service personal had been causing problems for the new government now based in Sacramento. Anyone that had military experience or law enforcement time were suspect of what was being called Constitutional Terrorists.

Travel was restricted, and food was being rationed as many farmers burned their crops creating shortages while the sitting Congress kept passing environmental laws making even growing food difficult.

Thomas did advise Bryon that there were ways of contacting people who might be able to locate Rhonda, but it was seldom used and risky. If they could get a message out they would, but to not expect much in results.

Later that afternoon, Adelle and Thomas sat with Bryon and explained the schedule for getting him back into shape after his experience in the sleep capsule. They would slowly increase his dietary intake as his stomach adjusted to the greater volume of food. Exercise would start with a simple treadmill as he once more built up his strength.

Neither could give Bryon a length of time to regain his strength but told him it was up to him as long as he did not overdue the exercise program and injure himself.

Six Months Later....

Bryon climbed down from the tractor after plowing a large path around the farm house and buildings as the wheat fields surrounding them were on fire, destroying the crop. He was now twelve pounds heavier than when he entered the capsule, but it was now all muscle. As he exercised to regain muscle tone, he continued to improve his own physical condition by pushing himself even further than he had in the Marine Corps. He had even begun to run up to five miles a day, up and down the dirt road leading to the farm house.

Adelle was taking blood samples every week and checking it in the small laboratory in the basement of the house. Every time he exercised on the weights in the barn, he was hooked to a biometric waist pack which recorded his vital signs and other aspects of his body he did not understand.

One thing that Thomas worked with him on was his intelligence. Thomas would ask him questions during the various times of the day, especially during the evening meal checking to see what he remembered. Bryon finally pushed the issue one evening why he was being asked questions about subjects he had never studied. Adelle finally explained that during his sleep period, he was being fed information on various subjects as if he had been taking college courses, and all Thomas was doing was to see if any of that data had been retained.

What Bryon never told either of them was that he was answering most of the questions wrong on purpose as he was aware that he had knowledge he did not have before going to sleep. This added to the feelings he had from awakening that something was wrong with what was happening to him. He just moved on from day to day waiting for the other shoe to drop. The one comfort was that he had his firearms at hand without restriction and always wore his revolver when working around the farm because of the rattlesnakes that were present on the high plains.

His hair was still long, over his shoulders which he kept in a ponytail and his beard was trimmed back to four inches below his chin. Bryon had yet to leave the farm other than to plow or hunt the doves that flew over the fields heading south with the farm's shotgun.

A month ago, he had been presented with a playmate. Adelle said it was to check his virility. She was young, petite and black. Tiara was her name and she claimed to be twenty years old, but she looked like she was barely fifteen. Thomas had returned with her during one of his fuel runs and said she had been hired by Doctor Browning just for this purpose. She had nothing with her except for the clothes on her back.

Tiara said she took the job because payment would pay for her education, but as Bryon would from time to time ask questions of her, it seemed she barely had a high school education. When he asked her about the outside world, she told him she had been forbidden to talk about it since her only purpose was to provide him with sex for the week she was there.

Adelle assured Bryon that Tiara was clean of any manner of STD's and that she was also protected against pregnancy. He was told that if Tiara did not suit him they would arrange for another girl to service him, so they could obtain the data they needed. When Bryon asked just how they would obtain such information, Adelle told him that Tiara would submit herself for examination each morning and from that exam, sperm samples would be taken for testing since sperm lived in a female's vaginal canal for days after depositing it.

Bryon had no problem with Tiara's race and as he had always been, he took this as something which he could not avoid. Their first coupling told him much about Tiara in that she was inexperienced, even if she was no longer a virgin. She tried hard to be a good lover to him and he used her as often as he wanted over the week she was there. Privately he kept thinking he had lost some control over his life as he felt using Tiara as often as did was not normal for him. He also never spoke to Adelle or Thomas that he seemed better equipped now to please a woman. Had they done something to him in hibernation to increase his manhood? The only comment Adelle made concerning this arrangement was that he was in fact very viral.

As nice a distraction Tiara was for that short time, Bryon was still confused about what had happened based upon the information Adelle and Thomas had given him. His mind had trouble adjusting the time frame with the decline in the country. There had been problems before he went to sleep, but the country was regaining its strength. He could not remember who the Vice-President had been when he went to sleep, but there was an election coming up at that time, so it was possible that was just information he did not have in his memory. There was no radio or television at the farm, and all its electrical power came from solar cells on the farm house roof or three small wind turbines.

Fuel for the farm equipment came from a supply of diesel which Thomas left with a small tank on the back of the one-ton flat-bed truck to refill as needed. Bryon had been told that without good papers, it was too dangerous for him to leave the farm. But today he wondered if leaving the farm would be all that difficult.

As he was walking to the barn a glimmer of something shining out in the wheat caught his attention. This was not the first time he had seen that glimmer today as he plowed the barrier between the farm and the fields. But sitting in a high tractor seat versus walking on the ground was two different things. He figured the object that was reflecting the sunlight was just something blown in by the winds as seen from the tractor seat but now it was seen from the ground.

Bryon entered the barn and went directly to the ladder up to the loft. He stayed in the shadows as he looked out the open loft door towards where the glimmer had come from. Bryon didn't need binoculars to notice the wheat being moved as if something was crawling through it towards the plowed barrier. Looking back towards the house, he noticed that the barn would obstruct Adelle and Thomas from seeing any action beyond the barn.

He checked the cheap watch he was given as the battery in the Breitling Rhonda had given him had died and there were no batteries available for it. Adelle should be in the kitchen about this time, preparing the evening meal. Thomas could be anywhere, but seldom left the house as he often helped Adelle in the kitchen.

After he slid down a rope, took another look at the house then the field before sprinting towards the wheat field. He made the wheat before he dropped to his knees inside the tall grain. Bryon got his bearings on the movement of the wheat and moved diagonally away from it in order to come at it from the side as they closed the distance to each other. His movements were slow as he listened for any sound that might give him an indication where the creature or individual was in relation to his own position.

Bryon heard a light metallic tick of metal on a rock to his left and shifted his position to listen for whatever was moving near him. He heard what he guessed was something being drug across the ground and moved to the sound. Bryon double checked to make sure the strap holding his revolver in his holster as he moved closer to the sounds of movement. As thick as the wheat was growing, he estimated he was about three feet from his target when he slowly rose up to check his position in relation to the movement of the stalks of grain.

His estimate was off by about a foot as the movement was a bit farther than three feet, but it was still close enough for him to make his move. Bryon stood up and looked at the body moving through the wheat. He was slightly behind the subject which placed him in the advantage for making his move. His target was completely covered in tan clothing and a small tan pack with a wrap on their hair, but the strains of black hair escaping from the wrap told him they had long hair, but not if it was male or female.

Bryon took one long step then dropped onto the back of the individual trapping them to the ground. He heard the individual grunt when he landed on top their back. Moving quickly, he moved so he could turn the person over and trap their arms. Once on their back he saw they were wearing dark wrap around glasses and the wrap went around their face, concealing who they were.

The subject fought him, but he was stronger and as soon as he had their arms trapped, he reached down and pulled the mask away from their face. Even with the glasses on he could tell this was a female with her figure hidden beneath the clothing and the equipment vest they were wearing. Bryon reached down and removed the glasses and took a good look at his captive and froze as he was looking at a face from his past.

"Rhonda?"

"Are you Bryon Petersen?" was the response to his question.

As much as this person looked like Rhonda, he realized she was younger than Rhonda was, or should be by this time.

"Who are you?"

"Are you Bryon Petersen, also once known as Bryon Reynolds?"

Bryon removed the restraining strap on his revolver and pulled it from its holster and pointed it at the female's face.

"Who told you about that name. About Bryon Reynolds?"

"My grandmother."

"Who is your grandmother?"

"Rhonda Petersen, and if you are Bryon Petersen, then you are my grandfather."

"Impossible."

"Please, are you Bryon Petersen?"

"Yeah, my name is Bryon Petersen, But, how can I have a granddaughter by Rhonda when I am only forty-seven years old? And it has only been four years since I last saw Rhonda."

"Grandfather, it has been fifty-two years since they put you in that sleep capsule. Grandmother Rhonda was pregnant with your son, Jacob at the time you went to sleep. I am Jacob's eldest daughter, Jocey. I can prove all of this if you will let me up, so I can get into my pack."

Bryon carefully slid off the girl's body keeping the revolver pointed at her.

"Don't get up but be damn careful what you pull out of that pack."

Jocey wormed around and got the pack off her back and laying on her stomach as she opened it. She pulled out a small video viewer, turned it on and faced it so Bryon could see it. The audio was not very loud, but Bryon had no problem hearing it as Rhonda came on the screen.

"Bryon my love, it has been five years since you went into the sleep capsule and I have returned as promised. The government decided considering your situation that they would continue the experiment for another five years."

Rhonda made a slight motion and a young child came into view and crawled up on her lap.

"Bryon, this is Jacob, your son. I was pregnant when you went to sleep. He is a wonderful child and he knows who you are as I have several photos of you while we were together. We'll

46

return in five years and hopefully they will let you out. I love you and wish for your safety."

The scene changed, and the video showed a much older Rhonda with a young man standing behind her.

"Bryon, it has been twenty years since you entered the experiment. They tell me that you are well, and everything is going better than first predicted. As you can see, Jacob has grown up and will go to the University of Nebraska this fall. I have not been with another man since you left, and I wait for you. I love you."

Once more the scene changed with Jacob in front of the camera.

"Father, Mother is gone. She had a heart attack, two months ago and never recovered. She waited for you, but the government kept you asleep. The world has changed drastically over the years."

A little girl came and stood in front of Jacob, looking at the camera.

"Father, this is Jocey, my daughter. She is learning about you as I was taught by Mother and if I cannot come for you, she will if possible. She is being taught the old ways of freedom even though the government has taken nearly all of our freedoms away for the years."

Jacob spoke for another ten minutes before the video ended with a photo of Jocey standing beside him.

Bryon looked at the photo then Jocey before holstering his revolver. Jocey placed the viewer aside then reached in and withdrew a plastic bag with papers in it and handed them to Bryon. He opened the bag and pulled the papers out and looked at them.

There was Jacob's birth certificate showing Bryon as his father. Then there was the birth certificate for Jocey, but the one document that upset him was Rhonda's death certificate. All the dates pointed to what Jocey had told him about how long he had been asleep.

"Jocey, let's say I buy all of this. Why didn't you just walk up to the front door and knock instead of this sneaking around?"

"Grandfather, do you have any idea who the people you are staying with actually are?"

"If what you say is true about how long I was asleep, then no."

"They are members of the Central Security Agency, the Secret Police, whose job is to put down any descent amongst the people. Do you remember your oath when you enlisted in the Marines?"

"Marines? I was never in the Marines. I was an Army Ranger."

"No Grandfather, you were a Marine and I can prove that. Grandmother was able to obtain everything your mother had on you when she passed away. There are photos and documents."

"Jocey, what is the purpose of changing my identity, my memories, in such a manner?"

"According to the information we were receiving from our inside person at the test site, they were feeding you information hoping to one, increase your intelligence, and two, to turn you into an assassin."

"Alright, who is this we you mentioned?"

"We have several names but the most common is the Resistance. We are resisting the loss of freedoms this country once had and the dictatorship that is destroying this land."

"Wait a minute. I understand there is a socialist government in place now, but a dictatorship?"

"Yes Grandfather, a dictatorship."

"Look, stop calling me Grandfather until I can confirm the fact. Bryon is fine with me. Now what is your place in this resistance?"

"I'm in Covert Intelligence."

"Covert as in how?"

"It's amazing what powerful men will talk about in bed, and I get paid a thousand dollars an hour to listen."

"You're a prostitute?"

"Yes Bryon, I am. But we have other concerns right now."

"Alright. What concerns are you talking about?"

"We're sitting in the middle of a wheat field and the only way I can convince you that I am your granddaughter is with a DNA test. Now I'm betting your hosts have a device that can do that, so we can get on with my mission."

"What is your mission?"

"To bring you in and hopefully deprogram you. Bryon, you have knowledge that can help our cause."

Bryon looked out over the wheat towards the barn then back at Jocey.

"I'm going to the barn to ensure that no one sees you when I signal you to move to it. Once in the barn you will hide while I go into the house and see if I can find some truth to what you are saying."

"Bryon, please be careful, those people are more than capable of killing you."

"Then why do they let me walk around armed?"

"Are you sure the bullets are real, or the revolver will even fire?"

Bryon thought about her question. He had not fired the revolver since he had awakened because he was unsure about getting more ammunition for it. He carefully looked towards the barn and house before getting up, taking one last look at the young woman lying in the dirt at his feet.

As he walked to the barn he kept thinking about what she had said about his upgraded intelligence and the questions he had been asked during the first weeks of his recovery. He knew answers to questions on subjects he had never studied or been interested in. As with many things since he awoke, something just did not feel right but he could not put a finger on what was bothering him.

At the barn, he stayed back in the shadows, watching the house before signaling Jocey to join him. As he was doing this, he also emptied his revolver, replacing the cartridges in it with ones from his belt loops at random intervals, then refilling the empty loops with the ones from his revolver. He considered test firing the revolver, but that would cause Adelle and Thomas to ask questions or cause them to be more cautious when he entered the house. He was going to play it by ear and hope for the best.

Jocey entered the barn and stayed in the shadows as she moved to him, then entered a stall and squatted down. He never spoke to her as he walked out of the barn towards the house. When he entered the back door at the kitchen, Adelle was at the sink cleaning vegetables for dinner. Thomas was nowhere to be seen, but access into the kitchen was wide open so Bryon positioned himself where he could cover the entrance to the kitchen.

"Adelle, I want to talk to Doctor Browning."

"What for, Bryon?"

"That's my business Adelle. Just find a way to arrange it please."

"Bryon, that's going to be difficult."

"Why? Is it because he's been dead for several years?"

"Why would you say that?"

"Because I was asleep longer than the time I was told. I want to talk to whoever it is you answer too, and I am not going to back down from that request."

Thomas entered the kitchen then with his right hand slightly behind his back.

"Adelle, I told you he was holding back on us."

As Thomas moved into the kitchen he began moving his right hand to the front of his body. In it he was holding a semi-automatic pistol. But before he could point it at Bryon, Bryon drew his revolver, thumbing back the hammer as he drew. Bryon had been practicing nearly every night in his room, getting his timing quicker and quicker in case he ever needed the big revolver.

"Thomas, I changed out the cartridges while in the barn. Shall we see if you tampered with all of my ammo?"

Thomas stopped the movement of his hand and then spread his hands out away from his body. Out of the corner of his eye, Bryon saw Adelle moving, swinging on him with the paring knife in her hand. Bryon stepped to her, blocking the arm with his left forearm preventing the knife from contacting him. Thomas started to bring his pistol back in line with Bryon when a sharp sound was heard to Bryon's right.

The sound Bryon heard was Jocey firing a tranquilizer dart into Thomas's chest. Adelle tried to recover, but Bryon put the muzzle of his revolver in her neck and held her there as he watched Thomas stagger back, then clutch at the dart before collapsing on the floor. Adelle dropped the paring knife just as Bryon heard a second loud sound closer and saw Adelle flinch. Suddenly her eyes seemed to glaze over, then roll back as she slumped to the floor.

Bryon turned to see Jocey holding an odd looking, four barreled pistol in her hand.

"What did you do?" He asked Jocey.

"Tranquilizer darts with a fast-acting sedative. But they are acting faster then I remember from the last time I used this thing. The lab techs must have increased the potency."

Jocey walked over to Thomas and picked up the pistol he had dropped and insured it was safe before laying it on the kitchen table.

"Give me a hand here. We have about thirty minutes before they wake up."

"What are you going to do?"

"Strip them naked and tie them to chairs, back to back. Come on, we're wasting time."

She was already working on stripping Thomas as Bryon moved to help her. As they got Thomas up in a chair, Bryon noticed numbers tattooed to Thomas's back at his right shoulder. He didn't think about them until he saw Adelle also had numbers in the same place. Jocey answered his unasked question as she was wrapping Adelle's legs to the chair legs with medical tape she had taken from her back pack.

"Those are their Democratic Socialists Membership Numbers. It proves they work for the government."

"Jocey, do you have any numbers tattooed on you?"

"No, and I'll strip nude if you want to check."

"No, you don't have too. So, what do we do now?"

"Let's go down into basement and see if our information was correct about them having a DNA analyzer down there."

Bryon had never been down in the basement as Thomas told him the equipment down there was old and delicate. Thomas explained if any manner of accident happened and the equipment was damaged, there was no repairing or replacing it. Bryon just took him at his word and stayed out of the basement.

After Jocey opened two doors with the keys she had taken off Thomas, it was obvious to Bryon the equipment was neither old, or delicate. Jocey only stood in the second door a couple of seconds before she homed in on an odd-looking machine on a table against the wall to her left.

Bryon stood back as he watched her first turn the power on the machine then put on a pair of latex gloves from a box on the table. Jocey pushed on two slots which sprang open with tiny trays extending out from the front of the machine. She then sterilized a pair of tweezers with alcohol and insured they were completely dry before she opened a plastic container marked as litmus paper and placed a single strip into each tray. Once in the trays, she picked up a bottle marked sterile water and placed several drops on each piece of paper before pushing the trays closed.

On the front of the machine was a small screen which Jocey activated, then using the buttons beside it scrolled through a menu of items until she selected 'cleanse' and activated the program. She turned to Bryon as the machine began to hum.

"Wash your hands, please."

Bryon just nodded then moved to a sink across the room and washed his hands using the liquid soap provided there. As he dried his hands on a folded towel near the sink, Jocey removed the latex gloves and washed hers. Once hers was dry, she put on another set of gloves and waited as the machine just hummed, then beeped twice.

Jocey opened the trays and carefully removed the litmus papers, then placed clean, dry strips into them. She picked up what Bryon recognized as a stick needle used by diabetics to prick their fingers and he watched as she took a sterile needle from a package and inserted it into the device, cocked it and handed it to him.

"It's set to stick you deeper than normal which is what we need to get sufficient blood for the test. Do a middle finger, then squeeze as much blood as possible onto either strip, but only on one strip. The other strip is for me."

As he did as she asked, she rigged another stick needle and once ready, she took off her left glove and pricked her finger. He fairly coated the paper in the tray he selected, then stood back as she did the same to the other piece of paper. Once she was satisfied, she used a gloved finger to push the trays closed. Again, she ran the menu until she selected 'DNA Comparison' from the menu and activated the program.

"You're pretty knowledgeable with that equipment."

She looked at Bryon and smiled.

"I should be, besides being a high paid whore, I'm also a board certified medical doctor. We have several of these machines in our clinic to run blood tests on patients. They are much better than having to draw blood and sending it out to a lab then waiting for hours or days for the results."

"You're a doctor?"

"Yes, I am. But because I'm not a party member, I can only work in clinics to help the poor. Or in my case, it's also a bordello and orphanage. No, I don't sell myself in the bordello, but I make house calls to some of the most powerful party members in the region. The money I make from that goes into the clinic and the information I often gain goes to the Resistance. My world is not the same one you once lived in, and we have to do what needs to be done to survive."

She just looked at Bryon and he could see that her eyes were watering up from exposing herself to him and that she did not like what she was doing. He did not know this woman in front of him, but he felt sorry for what she was having to live with if everything she had said was the truth. Neither spoke as the machine hummed in the background until it beeped twice. Jocey turned to it to collect the strip of paper that was being issued from it.

She read the paper, smiled then handed it to Bryon.

"Well Grandfather, here is the truth about who I am. It says I am one generation removed from you meaning I am your Granddaughter. And yes, I hate having to whore myself to help others."

Jocey handed him the strip of paper and it had the very information on it that she spoke of. She was directly related to him, and at one generation, she had to be his Granddaughter since he had no brothers or sisters to produce a niece.

"Alright Jocey, I'll accept this for now. What next?"

"Now we go talk to your keepers and fine out what they intended for you. On another side, I'm pleased that you accept who I am, but I'm also a bit disappointed."

As she was answering him, she was looking at some tool boxes on a shelf. She found the one she wanted and pulled it from the shelf.

"Disappointed? How so?"

"Tiara said you were fun in bed, if you were not my Grandfather, I'd want to find out. I may hate being a whore, but from time to time, sex is always fun."

"Tiara? You know her? And she said I was fun in bed? That girl barely knew how to act in bed."

"Tiara works in the clinic also and she is twenty-nine years old. When our pimp was contacted wanting a young, inexperienced girl to service a man at an isolated location for a week, we suspected it was you based on our intelligence. And don't get upset with the word pimp. He's actually our head of Intelligence."

"Is she also a doctor?"

"Yes, a Psychotherapist. She was evaluating you as she was sleeping with you. And she told me to tell you that she can't wait to see you again. Grandfather, I've done doubles with her on clients, you will enjoy meeting her in a neutral environment where she can be herself. She is wild in bed. Now let's go talk to your keepers."

Jocey headed for the doors with the tool box in her hand as Bryon followed, trying to get his head wrapped around this situation he suddenly found himself in. In the kitchen, they found both captives groggy and trying to clear their heads from the drug which knocked them out. Jocey put the tool box on the table with a loud bang causing them to look in the direction. She smiled at them before speaking.

"Both of you know what is in this tool box. Do I use it, or do you want to tell me what I want to know?"

"Fuck you bitch!" Thomas spat at her.

"Well, yes, I guess that answered my question." Jocey replied.

She turned to the table and opened the tool box, then removed a small electrical appliance with two knobs on it. She took the cord from it and moved around the table and stretched it to plug it into the wall socket above the kitchen counter. Back to the tool box, she removed a pair of long, thin wires and plugged them into the appliance.

Bryon just watched what she was doing and suspected this was a torture device using electricity. He did not like what he was seeing, but the fact that Thomas pulled a gun on him and Adelle tried to stab him with the paring knife removed most of the disgust he was feeling about what Jocey was doing.

Jocey took a small package from the tool box, opened it and moved in front of Adelle. From the package, she removed what Bryon recognized as a stick-on contact like used for EKGs, but it was larger than those. She stuck it on Adelle's inner thigh near her vagina. Bryon could see fear on Adelle's face.

He watched as Jocey took the long wires and connected one to the contact on Adelle's thigh then moved back to the tool box. From it she took another package, longer and slender than the previous package. She opened it and pulled a long, thin stainless-steel object from if the was turned up on one end and had a wire out the other.

Jocey moved in front of Adelle, kneeled in front of her and Bryon watched as she worked the object between Adelle's vaginal lips and from what he was seeing, turned the curved end into Adelle's vagina, then connected the other wire to the one extending from the object.

"Please don't do this." Adelle was pleading with Jocey.

"I don't have to do this if you answer all my questions."

"Shut up Adelle! Don't tell them anything!" Thomas yelled at her from behind.

Jocey laughed as she went back to the tool box and pulled out more wire and packages. She attached a contact to the inside of Thomas's thigh then opened another package which had an adjustable band in it. She grabbed Thomas's penis, pulled on it till

57

he cried out then wrapped the band around it. She connected the wires to them and moved back to the appliance and plugged them in.

"Grandfather, one thing I have learned is that for some reason, these socialist men all have small cocks."

She adjusted the dials on the appliance then turned it on. Adelle and Thomas screamed as the electrical current went through their genitals then she shut the appliance off.

"Now that was setting one for about three seconds, shall we try a higher setting for longer? Say a three setting for five seconds?"

"Jocey?"

"No Grandfather, stay out of this."

"Why do you keep calling him Grandfather?" Adelle gasped as she was trying to steady her breathing.

"Because he is my Grandfather. It's one of the best kept secrets concerning Bryon Petersen is that Rhonda Peterson had a son by him and I'm his daughter. But I'm not worried about you knowing that information. So, let's talk."

For the next hour, except when Jocey thought they were giving her bogus answers, she never touched the appliance. Bryon was amazed at how cold Jocey was as she questioned them then hit them with the current. The last time she shocked them, Thomas actually ejaculated from the effect of the current going through his genitals.

The purpose of Bryon being in this closed environment was to test him to see if the restructuring of his mind while in hibernation was effective. To see if the knowledge that had fed him had taken hold. If he passed the tests here, they would send him on to the next stage then out into the world to deal with those resisting the socialist government. If he failed, they would either kill him or return him to the laboratory for further study.

They had not replaced the cartridges in his revolver and allowed him to wear it to make Bryon feel comfortable with his environment, so he would not question his own freedom. When Jocey asked how they had planned on killing Bryon, she was told they would introduce a poison gas into his room at night if they felt they had to kill him.

When Jocey had all the information she felt she needed, she removed a small, black zippered bag from her pack and laid it out on the table. From it she removed a vial with a bright blue liquid in it and a syringe. She drew up a dose into the syringe then went to Adelle and stuck her inside her thigh, pushing the liquid into her body.

"It's not poison Adelle, it's something to relax you so we can do what we need to do, then give us time to get away. Killing you is an option, but not today."

"Thank you." Adelle muttered.

Jocey drew a second dose and did the same to Thomas, then stood back after she put the syringe and vial back into the pouch and closed it up. No one spoke as Jocey watched as first Adelle, then Thomas went to sleep. Jocey stepped to Adelle, slapped her with no response then did the same to Thomas getting the same response or no response from him. She started untying Thomas as she spoke.

"Grandfather, we have roughly twelve hours to search the house for anything linking you to them and clear out of here before they wake up."

"Jocey, aren't you afraid all they will do is notify their bosses and hunt you down as they hunt me down?"

"No, because when they wake up, they won't even know their own names. That is an amnesia drug and there is no antidote for it. Let's move them to their bed, then while you pack your things up, I'll search the basement for records and video recordings, especially the ones of you having sex with Tiara."

Bryon chuckled.

"I figured they were recording those sessions. Do you think they may have sent copies out already?"

"That's a risk we have to take. Tiara has already gone through facial reconstruction and had her prints adjusted so it'll be difficult to get a quick ID of her when they start investigating this situation once they come to investigate why these people have not reported in after a few days."

They moved Adelle and Thomas to their bed then Bryon went to pack. Jocey told him to just take his bags to the front door for now and when ready, to come to the basement with a pair of pliers. After he staged his things at the front door, he went out to the tool crib in the barn for a pair of pliers before joining Jocey in the basement.

Jocey was busy copying all the computer records on Bryon as he just stood back and watched. Once she was happy she had copies of everything, she ran a program from a thumb drive she had, wiping clean the computer's hard drive. She then wiped down the entire room with an alcohol-soaked rag, then went to the medical room and did the same. She commented that if they had the means, they would strip the medical room for the equipment and use it elsewhere for the good of the people, but there was no time to make those arrangements. When she locked the doors in the basement, she left the key in the lock and had Bryon snap it off in the lock with the pliers, ruining the lock.

She went through the house collecting all manner of things, especially the identification cards and such on Adelle and Thomas.

It took her a couple attempts to get the safe opened that she found in the bottom of their closet, and from it she removed all the money and other documents from it, leaving nothing for others to find.

Jocey handed Bryon a packet from the safe containing his identification cards and passport. She told him they would still be good for at least twenty-four hours which would be enough time to get to Denver, then they could build a new identification for him.

When she was done, she told Bryon they had just over two hours before it would be safe for them to leave without being observed by satellite. She had him fix something to eat since his prints would be all over the house. As they ate, he asked her questions about her life, her father, and about how Rhonda had lived before her death.

As the clock slowly moved the hours forward, Jocey pulled a small radio from her pack, activated it and pressed the push-to-talk button three times and waited. She received three breaks of the squelch and smiled at Bryon.

"Our ride will be here in a few minutes. Let's get ready for them."

As they waited for their ride, he remembered once reading about female doctor's, professionals, in Venezuela, who had turned to prostitution to survive in their Socialists environment back around 2017 or so. History repeating itself in another location? Didn't a liberal female once predict that women would have to whore themselves to survive due to global warming? But the weather was mild, nothing like the global warming once predicted. Again, he had the feeling something was wrong with the situation he had found himself in.

Denver

A battered crew cabbed pick-up arrived at the farm house to collect Bryon and Jocey. The back of the truck was filled with cartons of vegetables and they moved them around and laid his bags on the bed along with Bryon's firearms, then covered them up with the cartons. Jocey explained that the police were too lazy to look under the cartons, but if they looked into the cab and saw his firearms, they would be in big trouble since it was illegal to own a firearm now that the socialist had taken control.

The ride to Denver was uneventful as no one talked during the two-hour long drive to the city. Jocey had stripped of the clothes she had been wearing while waiting for the truck, changing into clothes that were worn and looked to have been worn while harvesting the vegetables. Bryon noticed she was covered in exotic and erotic tattoos but decided to ask about them later when alone.

As they drove downtown into Denver, Bryon noticed that half the street lights were not on and at some street intersections, the lights did not work but stop signs were in place to control traffic. Bryon had been to Denver many times delivering loads and thought the city was attractive, but now, it looked like a dump.

When they pulled into a covered parking area of a large hotel, Jocey told Bryon this was once the Hilton Garden Inn hotel. Except for the restaurant area of the ground floor, the rest of the ground level had been converted into their clinic. The next two floors were their orphanage. The fourth and fifth floors were living spaces for staff and those folks that worked for the clinic out on the streets of Denver. The Seventh floor was reserved for those seeking a night of sexual relief with the partner they brought with them while the ninth floor was their bordello. The large suite at the top was reserved for parties, orgy's if the client could afford the price.

Bryon was taken to the fifth floor and given the corner room overlooking Welton Street and 15ᵗʰ Street. Jocey explained that the only reason this building had working elevators was because of the bordello since their clients were on the average high-ranking party officials who did not like walking up stairs. He was told to use the staircase to avoid running into those people.

It surprised Bryon that the room was well maintained, cleaned and the towels and linen were as if this hotel was still owned by the Hilton's back when he was still a free man.

Jocey gave him a kiss on the cheek and told him she had to go to work and would talk to him later. He gave her a look she only smiled at, then told Bryon she was going to work in the clinic, not a bedroom. If he was hungry, just go to the restaurant and they would fix him something.

Bryon changed out of the clothes he had been wearing all day after a short, hot shower, then tried the television in the room. It worked which surprised him, but the programming was limited, and it seemed even the game shows were politically inclined to socialist propaganda.

He thought about going down to get something to eat when there was a knock on his door. Jocey had not told him to open his door so he went to see who it might be. Opening the door, he found a petite, dark skinned female with Asian looks smiling at him.

"Can I help you?" He asked.

"Certainly Bryon. You can invite me in and we can pick up where we left off at the farm."

"Tiara?"

"I was, but now call me Ciara. Sort of a play on my old name but easier to me to remember. Well, do I come in or go upstairs and wait for someone to pay me to do what I want to do with you for free?"

Bryon invited her in and quickly discovered Jocey was right about her being wild in bed as he also noticed her breasts were larger than he remembered. She was in no hurry getting to the end game and made it interesting getting there.

He woke up to someone knocking on his door with Ciara lying across him. Bryon eased out from under her, pulled his trousers on and went to see who was at the door. Looking through the peep hole he saw it was Jocey. Opening the door, he saw she had a cart with her.

"What time is it?" He asked her.

"Just after six, I figured you'd need something to boost your energy after a night with Ciara."

"Yeah, you were right about her. Well, come on in and let's see what you brought the condemned man."

"Condemned? What's that mean?"

"Jocey, between the people we left at the farm and Ciara, I'm not sure how long I have left in this world."

Jocey laughed.

"At least with Ciara, you'll die happy."

He stepped out of the way allowing Jocey to move the cart into the room finding Ciara sitting up in bed, uncovered and exposing herself.

"I heard that Bryon. You might die happy but if we keep this up, a normal man won't be able to please me." Ciara commented.

Jocey laughed.

64

Bryon just shook his head as he moved to the cart to see what was under the covered dishes. Scrambled eggs and ham with home fries. He fixed a plate and went to the desk to eat. In the mirror over the desk he noticed that Jocey had sat down on the bed and Ciara was wrapped around her kissing her. He was staring into the mirror when they broke the kiss and Jocey looked at him.

"Yes, Grandfather, I go both ways. If you weren't my grandfather, I'd be out of these clothes playing with Ciara as you ate, then drag you to bed. But I think I like the idea of you being my Grandfather more than the thought of a lover."

"Jocey, Ciara, do me a favor please. Keep your personal relationship out of my sight just so my thoughts do not get corrupted. I'm still trying to get use to having a Granddaughter and especially one that looks so much like her Grandmother."

Jocey moved off the bed.

"Sorry Grandfather. You did love Grandmother Rhonda, didn't you?"

"Yes, I did, and it hurts that I never told her. Now to change the subject, what happens now?"

Ciara answered his question.

"Bryon, the first thing is to change your appearance such as mine has been changed to protect you while building a new identification for you. One that will pass detection. Then we or myself and my team will see how deep your programming has gone and try to fix it. Once we are satisfied, then you can make your own decisions about what to do with the rest of your life. Join us or move on."

"That's a high-risk situation for you isn't it? I mean I'll know about this place and all of you. How will you know that I won't be caught and tell everything I know?"

"Grandfather, we face that situation daily. We had two choices with you. Kill you or what we are planning to do. But we could not allow you out, under their influence to kill members of the Resistance."

"How do you know I'm not playing you right now, to get to the top of the Resistance so I can kill them?"

"Grandmother wrote in her private journal that deep in your nature, your psychological make-up lay an innate sense of right and wrong. That you would never harm anyone just because you were ordered too."

"Jocey, my memories they have corrupted said I was an Army Ranger and have killed dozens of people. You said I was actually a Marine. What does that past have to say about me?"

"Yes, according to your service records, you have killed, and was even wounded once. But that experience and the experience that lead you to Rhonda has deep roots in you. Yes, Grandfather you are capable of killing, but not just because someone points a finger and says you should."

Ciara added to the conversation.

"Bryon, you killed to protect yourself and the men around you. The Socialists Progressives have this odd thinking in that all men who become soldiers are killers and can be guided to kill on order. But we also know they have a couple of men, psychopaths, who are being treated who would do that, and enjoy doing it. To be completely honest with you, if the time comes, it has been discussed sending you after those people only, not those that control them. We can remove the controllers, but without them, the psychopaths would be free to do what they want, when they want and too they want. We'll make no demands on you, only ask that you consider the possibility."

Bryon looked at the women then back at his plate of cooling food.

"I need to think about this." As he turned back to continue eating. In the mirror he saw Jocey give Ciara a quick peck on the lips then came to him and gave him a wet kiss on his cheek, then left without saying another word.

Later when he showered, Ciara joined him and took him with her mouth in the shower. After she dried off, she gave him a long, wet kiss, then left him to his thoughts.

Ciara reminded him that he had no emotional ties to Jocey since he had no knowledge of her until a few days ago. He remembered one of his female cousins that as nice looking as she was, the thought of having sex with her never crossed his mind as they grew up together, but another cousin he had never met until he was fifteen made him envision her nude body lying on his bed waiting for him.

A family is grown respecting their place in it and when something breaks, something that respects family, then a father might rape his daughter, or granddaughter. Something is weak in a man who would do such a thing. He had no emotional ties to Jocey and she was desirable, but she was still his Granddaughter by DNA. A tear came to his eye as he hated that he never saw his son, Jacob becoming a man, or held tiny Jocey as a baby.

But without the program which saved his life, he would not even have Jocey in his life. Bryon found pride in that she was a medical doctor, but within that pride was developing a hatred for those who drove her to prostitution to fund the clinic she worked in. He told himself that alone was a reason to go after those that forced their ideals on others as they took their freedoms away from them.

Bryon turned the television on to get a better grasp of the propaganda being telecast. To him it was obvious what was being preached to the masses was complete nonsense, but his memories were corrupted with the information force fed into him while in hibernation, and he recognized that those memories needed to be erased.

It dawned on him that the commercials for sex aides or sexual disease prevention not only showed nude adults utilizing those items while having actual sex on camera, quick flashes of other users during the commercials seemed to portray even younger users. Somewhere in his mind he had the feeling he should be upset about such content on normal programming channels where children could view it.

Just before twelve, he went down to the restaurant to eat and maybe find Jocey or Ciara. Instead he was approached by a man in a white lab coat that was about his age, or the age he went into the program.

"Bryon, I'm Doctor Prescott. May I sit down?"

"Sure, go ahead."

"Bryon, I do the plastic surgery around here. When do you think you will be ready for some adjustments to change your appearance?"

"I'll leave that up to you since it seems I have no place to go and all of the time in the world not to get there."

Prescott laughed.

"I don't think we'll have to do much to you as you have a fairly neutral look now. But we will have to do enough adjusting so facial recognition will not tag you as Bryon Petersen. Once you have finished eating, I'd like to take you back to my office, take a couple photos of you and work out how we are going to change your looks."

"Sure, why not. Let me ask you something first. I was watching television before I came down here and some of the commercials were sexually explicit, or was I watching a closed channel?"

"No, that is all over the channels now. Keep the public distracted with sex and they won't noticed how screwed they really are."

"Some of the actors in those commercials seemed awful young."

"Too young. It's why we have an orphanage upstairs. We are the only medical clinic in Denver that will not perform abortions. Those clinics get large government grants, while we get to have electricity because of the orphanage, and our donations of food are not messed with, otherwise, without the bordello, we would have trouble keeping both the clinic and the orphanage open."

"So, the social mores of the country have gone into the gutter Doctor?"

"I'm not familiar with that term, into the gutter, but since trash gets washed away into gutters, I suppose that fits."

"You have a good grasp of the meaning Doc. Alright, I'm done here, let's go see about a new face."

After several photographs were made and uploaded into Doctor Prescott's computer, he adjusted Bryon's face and asked for Bryon's opinion. Bryon finally told Prescott to let Jocey pick a face she would be happy with as his Granddaughter, then he left for his room.

Over the next week, Jocey spent as much time with Bryon as she had available talking about her father and brother. Her father, Jacob taught engineering at the University of Nebraska. Simon, her younger brother was finishing up his degree in Horticulture, also at the University of Nebraska. Her mother had left when Simon was five to live in a commune in Utah and they had not seen her since. Her father knew what Jocey was doing and supported her, but her brother was kept out of the picture other than that she worked in a medical clinic.

When Bryon asked about her tattoos, Jocey said that some of her sex clients could get rough and the tattoos hid any bruising or marks on her body. They were not allowed to mark her neck or face, but she also charged them more for their brutality. They were also prohibited from scaring her. Jocey said those that were rough also had small penises. They had to prove their manhood by dominance since they couldn't in bed. They also tended towards anal sex since at least the anus was tight on their small cocks.

Bryon was amazed she could speak about her sexual activities as if it was someone else, not her own experiences. He asked how they controlled sexually transmitted diseases and pregnancies within the bordello and their outside activities.

Jocey explained that each sex worker had an implant to prevent pregnancy, but each morning after being active, they took a morning after pill to insure no pregnancies. Also, each client entering the bordello was first checked for STD's which utilized a smaller version of the machine which did the DNA check before they were allowed to engage with one of the girls or boys.

Yes, they had young men who worked upstairs servicing their female clients and a few men who preferred men. Every individual who serviced a client was checked for STD's the next morning to insure the checks made the night before were still accurate and effective.

This answered several other questions in his mind since during the week, he had been visited by other young ladies who spent the night with him and they never required him to use a condom. They were a mixture of races; white, black, Mexican, Asian, all fit with modest breasts. None of those girls were under the age of eighteen according to what they told him, and even though he felt something was wrong about using them, he just went along, and he had to admit he enjoyed the sex. But something was still not as it should be in his mind.

70

Ciara returned to him on the sixth night and exhausted him before they both fell asleep. She told him that the next morning, they were going to restructure his face based on what she and Jocey thought he should look like.

Before he fell asleep he had this feeling that he never had as many sexual partners before over a short period of time. He had asked Jocey about the girls coming down from the bordello to service him and she just smiled and told him to enjoy it. But that was part of his problem, he was enjoying the attention and action, maybe too much.

A New Look

Bryon woke to the smell of disinfectant and bright lights. His last memory was of Jocey introducing a drug into his IV as she was assisting in the surgery on his face. He could feel the bandages on his face and as he tried to move his arms, he felt them tied down, restrained, preventing him from touching his face.

"Be still Bryon, if you feel any pain, we can give you something for it."

The voice he heard belonged to Ciara. He tried to talk but the bandages prevented much movement of his jaw and mouth.

"I'm alright." He muttered.

"Good, now just be still and try to go back to sleep. You're in recovery for now, later we'll move you up to your room."

"Okay." He once again muttered.

The next time he woke, he was being moved off the gurney onto his own bed. He just let the people moving him deal with all the problems and tried to relax. Bryon could feel the catheter in his penis and the sheet he was lying on felt funny until he realized it was a plastic sheet in case he crapped on himself while in this condition.

Time has no meaning when in such a position and he could only measure it by someone feeding him malted drinks or warm soup broth through a straw as he lay on the bed. His sheet was changed as needed and he was given a sponge bath each time including washing his ass as if he was a baby.

Although they never talked, he knew there was someone always in the room with him cause if he asked for a drink of water, a straw was soon introduced to his mouth, so he could drink. He did ask for some soft music to listen too, so he would not feel isolated and sometime later he heard music playing from across the room.

Jocey often came to his room to talk to him, telling him what was happening in the world outside the hotel. She removed the IV's, then a few days later she removed the catheter for him and remarked about his size saying Ciara was one lucky girl. But other than only touching him to remove the catheter, she never touched him again.

From then on if he had to use the bathroom, whoever was with him guided him to it and insured he was clean afterwards. Bryon felt like an invalid, but understood that until his bandages could be removed, he was a victim of his situation.

Twice Doctor Prescott came and removed his bandages to check on his work, then rebandaged him to protect the work until it was healed enough to go without. His eyes were bandaged because of the work around the eyes, otherwise he would not have had to keep them bandaged.

Almost two weeks after the surgery, Prescott removed the bandages and announced his work complete with no noticeable scaring. When Bryon looked into the mirror, once again a stranger looked back at him. This time his features were more American Indian to match his skin tone instead of the features of his half German, half Cherokee mother.

During the time he was unable to do more than lie around while waiting for the bandages to be removed, he took that time to consider his situation. As enjoyable as the sex had been, it was too easy. Was he being played while in bed or was there something now embedded in his mind that wasn't there before? He tried hard to remember his life before going into hibernation, but it was difficult. Then he wondered why they left the memories of Rhonda intact?

When he had a knock on his door that evening he had decided that he was going to send them away, but looking through the peep hole, he saw Ciara standing in the hall dressed for the evening. He opened the door.

"What's up Ciara?"

"Jocey and I have an engagement tonight and I wanted to come by and see your new face before we left. Damn, you turned out better than we figured. If I didn't have this engagement, I'd be all over you right now."

"Ciara, do the two of you have to do this?"

"Bryon, tonight will pay for a new x-ray which we really need. If we could get it another way, I wouldn't be dressed like this and neither would Jocey. I've got to go now. Would you like me to have a girl come down to take care of you tonight?"

"No, and post a note that if I wish company, I'll call upstairs for it. Until then, leave me alone."

He stepped back into the room and closed the door before Ciara could say another word. As tempted as he was to look out the peep hole, he just went to the couch and dropped down on it, thinking he had been a bit harsh at the end with Ciara, but he only said what he felt. He liked Ciara, maybe too much at this juncture in his life.

Bryon had discovered that he was becoming comfortable with the environment he was in and still did not know how things would end up. He found himself hating what was happening and as things happened before in his life, it seemed he had no control over his life. But he had the odd feeling that no matter where he was, what time of the day it was, he felt he was being watched.

Two days later Bryon helped off-load a new x-ray machine and move it into place. Jocey barely looked at him and when she did she had a look of embarrassment on her face. He finally walked over to her and kissed her on the forehead.

"I hate what you are doing but I understand why. Tell whomever is going to try to undo my conditioning to get busy, I'm tired of waiting."

Raping the Psyche

Ciara came for Bryon a couple hours later and took him into the basement of the hotel into a padded room where there was a cot, a table, and chair. She had him strip to his underwear and told him to lay down on the cot as she left to get what she needed for this treatment session as she called it.

She returned with a medical bag and a helper who brought a machine in with him, placed it on the table then left them alone. Ciara did not speak to him as she got things ready on the table then came to him to place a contact headband on his head. Bryon reached up and gently grabbed her arm.

"Ciara, the other night. I came off too harsh with you. I'm sorry."

"Sorry for being harsh, or sorry for what you said?"

"Both. I don't know who the real me is anymore. Find him and maybe we can go from there."

Ciara leaned over and gave him a short kiss, then went back to work. Once she had him hooked up to her machine, she filled a syringe, went to him and gave him an injection inside his elbow. Ciara never spoke to him as she did this and then she moved away, back to the table and sat down as she waited for the drug to take effect. Bryon just tried to relax, then suddenly the drug took effect and for him, the lights went out.

Bryon awoke covered in sweat and feeling like he had just ran five miles with a heavy pack on. He looked to his left for Ciara, but she was gone, replaced by one of the men who worked around the clinic.

"Bryon, I'm here to help you back to your room when you think you are up to taking the walk."

When Bryon tried to sit up, it felt as if his head was going to come apart from the movement, and his throat was sore.

"Damn," He croaked out, "What the hell did she give me?"

"It's a psychotropic drug, designed to break down the barriers caused by what is commonly called brainwashing."

"How did I do?"

"I have no idea. Doctor Ragsdale brought me in after she was done for this session. You'll have to ask her."

"Ragsdale?"

"Yes, Ciara, you didn't know her last name?"

"No. Let's see if I can get up and get out of here."

It took some effort on Bryon's part to sit up then after a moment, stand up on wobbly legs.

"What's your name?" Bryon asked.

"David. I have a wheelchair outside if you need it, so all we have to do is make it out there. The padded floor makes it hard to use it in here."

"Right now, just standing is hard. Give me a hand, will ya?"

David helped him to the out the door and into the wheelchair. From there to the elevator up to Bryon's room, where David deposited him on his bed. Bryon lay still, trying not to cause anymore ache in his body as his mind seemed to bounce from one character to another in his head. The mix of his real self and the one planted into his head was confusing.

He had no idea how long he lay there when there was a knock on his door, then it opened with one of the girls from upstairs entering, pushing a room service cart. She was fully clothed and once she had the cart out of the way, she helped Bryon up and to his desk chair. She hardly spoke to him other to give him basic instructions as she set food and drink on the desk, then moved out of his way so he could eat. The food was soft, and barely spiced which Bryon was grateful for as his stomach rebelled against eating.

When he had eaten all that he felt he could tolerate, she asked him if he needed to use the bathroom. He said it might be a good idea and she helped him to get there and then helped clean himself afterwards. He felt like an infant having to be helped in such a manner.

After she had him back on the bed, and the desk cleaned off she smiled at him.

"Bryon, once you feel up to it, I'd like to spend a night in that bed with you. Just call for Megan, and if I'm not already engaged, I'll be right down."

"Thank you, Megan, but the way I feel right now, I doubt I'll ever be able to get an erection again."

She laughed as she left the room, leaving him once again to his thoughts. He finally fell asleep and for the first time since his awakening from hibernation, he had nightmares.

Ciara sat in the room next to his watching via a hidden camera as he thrashed on the bed during his nightmares. Jocey and Doctor Prescott were also there watching and listening to his screams and cries to men long dead as his real memories clashed with the ones implanted into his mind.

Jocey wanted to go to him, comfort him, but Ciara refused to allow it.

"Jocey, if you go in there now, he'll most likely rape you. I use the term rape because even if you give yourself to him, that is how he will view it later on, and that can damage him worse than he already is. You look too much like your Grandmother and that's what he will see, not his Granddaughter."

"Is Megan at risk being near him in this state?"

"No, and even if he did take her, she is not you. He has no ties to her, but you heard him say he doubted he could even get an erection. But if you went to him, you'd end up on the bed, holding him, comforting him, then all bets are off what he might be able to do. Part of his programming removed or covered up his natural inhibitions towards sex."

"I understand Ciara, but it hurts to see him suffer like that."

"Once his treatment is complete, he won't have such violent nightmares. Believe me, of all the people I have treated in this manner, this hurts me to watch too."

"I know Ciara. You're in love with him, aren't you?"

"Yes, I am. Now get out of here, it's going to be a long night as it is. Jim, you have anything to say?"

Doctor Prescott was quiet for a moment before answering.

"Ciara, if it wasn't for the fact you are good at what you do, and the only game in town for us, I'd remove you from this case. Do not allow your personal feelings to get in the way here. We need him intact, and able to function, not a basket case."

"I know Jim. I'll keep it professional until finished, but after that, all bets are off."

"I know you'll keep it professional, but for the record, be damn careful. And from the looks of you, that session played hard on you too, so get some rest, you still have much to do with him."

"Yes, Doctor Prescott, I shall."

Ciara watched him until his nightmares went away and he fell into a deep sleep. She set the alarm next to the room's bed and laid down knowing if he cried out again during the night, she would be awoken from the sounds coming through the speakers. Her own dreams were not pleasant that night and the alarm woke her before she was ready.

The next morning, Megan woke Bryon up when she brought him breakfast.

"You look tired Megan." Bryon spoke as he slowly walked to the desk to eat.

"I had a long night. I'll get some rest today after we get you back down for your next session."

Bryon understood what she meant by a long night but never approached the subject. He just ate what he felt he could while drinking the carafe of coffee dry. Megan once again helped him in the bathroom, making no further comment about joining him in bed, and left him waiting for David to come for him.

The first thing he noticed when he entered the padded room was the equipment on the table had changed. Large and more complex. Ciara was there, preparing the wiring harness from the machine, untangling it as she stretched it out to the cot. He noticed that she also looked as if she also had a long night but told himself not to make any statement or inquiries concerning such.

He did ask if the drug she was giving him caused his weakness which she confirmed it did, but once they complete the treatment, he would regain his strength and vitality.

Bryon endured six treatments overall until Ciara told him he was as cured as he would ever be and that from time to time, planted memories may crop up, but he would be able to distinguish those memories from his real ones. He noticed that Ciara looked ragged each morning as she was not getting much rest but did not inquire of her about what she was doing at night. When he commented to David that it seemed Ciara was burning the candle at both ends, dealing with him and taking clients, David told him she was off rotation and had not taken a contract since she started his treatment. He never asked what she was doing to look so tired.

Each day Megan brought him breakfast and dinner as he was in treatment during the day. On the final day, after he had eaten his evening meal, she went down on him as he sat in the desk chair knowing Ciara would be watching from the other room. Once finished, Megan helped him to bed, cleaned up the desk and left smiling at him.

The next morning, Bryon had his photo taken for a new set of identification papers and he chose the name Ryan Westbrook as his new name. Later that morning, Ciara came to visit him in his room, to further discuss his treatment and possibilities. She was wearing slacks and a white lab coat and had him sit on the couch as she took the stiff chair from the desk.

"For this session, I'm still going to refer to you as Bryon, since it effects those memories."

"Sure, no problem Ciara. Where do we start?"

"Who is or was Mark Collins?"

"He was my Company Commander in the Seventh Transportation Battalion in Iraq."

She asked nearly a dozen similar questions before he asked one of his own.

"Ciara, these people you keep asking me about are from my real life, but where did you get those names?"

"Jocey provided them from the items Rhonda retrieved from your mother's estate."

"That's right, Mom had nearly all of my Marine things because I never got around to moving them to my house after I built it. I had forgotten about that."

Ciara changed directions and asked questions concerning his hibernation education which surprised Bryon that he still retained that information, including what was considered his Army Ranger Training. He asked how she managed to leave that in his mind while removing the identity the Socialists had placed in there.

"Bryon, I'm not supposed to tell you this, but I will. That machine I had you hooked to in the treatment room was also hooked to me once you were unconscious. It allowed me to actually enter your mind, to walked through it if you care to look at it that way, and remove the things needed to be removed. I spent days, weeks, reading the files on you that Jocey had, from your school year books, to the journals kept by Rhonda. Her journals were both professional concerning your case, and the private one she kept on you. I used those as a guide along with a few other things we acquired to in a sense, to rape your psyche."

He sat for a long time, looking at her as she held no emotion on her face.

"Did you implant the feelings I have for you while inside my head?"

"No Bryon, I did not. That would have been unethical of me. I felt those feelings as I was in there and I left them alone. But I will not lie to you, those feelings played hard on me, and it was tempting to remove them."

"Why would you want to remove them?"

"Bryon, I have said too much, please can we move on?"

"Ciara, was it because you were connected to me that you looked so tired every morning?"

"Yes, as I said, being connected to you played hard on me, I felt your pain as if it was my own. It's part of the risk I must take when using that machine to connect myself with a patient. But I'll be alright in a couple of days, so ease your mind about me."

"Alright. What now?"

"The drugs we had to give you played havoc on your body as you well know, but in a couple of days, you'll return to normal, or as normal as possible. Tomorrow, David will show you the exercise room in the basement and you need to start getting back in shape. You've lost over ten pounds during the treatment, so eat well and regain your strength."

"Okay, that makes sense. Next?"

"The word has been passed on to everyone here about your new name and once I leave this room, Bryon Petersen will cease to exist. Get used to being called Ryan, it will help keep you out of trouble later. I have to go now, but we can talk more tomorrow. Would you like for me to send Megan down to spend the day and night with you?"

"I'd rather you stayed."

Ciara stood and just looked at Bryon.

"I can't. I have an engagement this evening."

"No way I can talk you out of it and stay here?"

"Bryon, this will be a very profitable night. A husband and wife engagement, a threesome if you will. With that money we can buy medicines we need for the clinic, and a few minor items we also need. I didn't take this contract earlier because I was working with you, so I can't cancel. I'm sorry, but this is how we are forced to live until changes can be made to the outside world."

Bryon could see tears forming in her eyes as she spoke, then she turned away, walked to the door and closed it behind her. He got up from the couch and moved to the windows to look out over Denver, seeing the decay brought about by small people desiring power beyond their ability.

"Alright," He thought, "He was a man out of his own time. A man who knew things and had the ability to execute them. How much good he could do he was uncertain of, but he would try, even if he never would be able to have Ciara all to himself."

He went to the phone, called upstairs and asked for Megan to come down.

A New Name and Purpose

Megan nearly ran into his room and from her first words, his new name was established. She only referred to him as Ryan as she tended to his desires. Desires he would have rather shared with Ciara. Even as weak as he felt, he had no problem dealing with Megan in bed. Ryan looked over at Megan laid out on her back the bed, uncovered and asleep thinking as enjoyable as it was, something in the back of his mind still told him this was wrong.

He learned she was nineteen and had come to the clinic when she was fifteen, already experienced and turning tricks to live. One of the clinic's street workers, individuals who tended to the needs of the homeless with food and medicines, had spotted her and brought her in. She had yet to catch an STD, and was not pregnant, but that was only a matter of time.

Megan had worked in the kitchen, earning her keep until she was seventeen, when she asked to work upstairs. It was known she was still having sex with some of the younger males at the clinic during her off hours, so she was allowed to move upstairs.

It had been an interesting night as Megan was well versed in bed and the noise she made came from deep inside of her, not fake as she was working to please a client. Ryan felt guilty as he dressed in loose clothing to go exercise. Did he call for Megan out of spite because Ciara was going out to fill a contract with her body? He never touched Megan or spoke to her as he left the room to start his new life.

He found David in the clinic who took him down to the exercise room. The equipment was old but well maintained and Ryan as he now thought of himself, started with an incline treadmill and spent a half hour on it before moving to the old Bow-Flex where he pushed himself on different exercises for nearly two hours, building up weights and number of repetitions, until he knew he was peaked out.

After he decided he had enough for the day, he went up to the restaurant for something to eat before going back to his room to shower and think.

Think. He had too much time on his hands to think. In a way it was like driving a truck except part of his mind had to stay focused on his driving, but now, there was nothing to focus on. He was becoming a prisoner of his own thoughts.

In the restaurant, he was told that Doctor Prescott had order a high protein diet for him to help rebuild his strength. He ordered a small steak and eggs with fried potatoes. Ryan understood that beef was not readily available to the staff and was hesitant to order it but knew he needed the protein if he was to do anything to help these people.

As he ate, he noticed Megan sitting across the dining room with four other girls from upstairs. From time to time, one of the girls would look over at him and he knew that taking Megan to his bed had been a mistake in more ways than her age.

He finished his meal, then went to his room, locking the door behind him so he would not have a visitor walking in on him. But he soon felt claustrophobic and even looking out the windows did not help.

Ryan knew he could not go outside and walk around since he did not have his papers yet, then thought about going up to the roof. He left his room, locking it behind him and went to the stairs to go up to the roof. His concern was meeting one of the girls from upstairs in the stairwell as he went up the stairs.

On the roof he found what looked like a patio with bed frames spread about without mattresses. He just shook his head figuring this was for a party, an orgy under the stars. Ryan walked over to the edge of the roof and looked down at the streets below him. What people that were moving around seemed to move without any purpose. This was not the Denver he remembered,

86

and he knew he had to do something about that situation even at the cost of his own life. His oath taken upon enlistment in the Marine Corps came back to him. He moved away from the edge of the roof and sat on a bed frame to consider his situation.

Ryan sat thinking about the enemy which caused his Granddaughter to prostitute herself to help others. An enemy which caused a woman he felt he was falling in love with whore herself to buy medicines for homeless. An enemy that forced young girls who should be reading teen magazines, or going to parties and proms, instead of spreading their legs to pay for their keep.

Now all he needed was clear targets to exercise the knowledge they had given him. His Marine training was good, but the Ranger training they had planted into his brain was even better. He first had to improve his own physical condition, then hopefully Jocey and the others could point him at targets he could remove which would hopefully cause her condition to improve.

He also recognized that no matter how well Ciara had cleared his mind of the person put inside of him during hibernation, he was not the same man he once was. For the first time in his life, in his memories, he learned to hate. Hate the system which put him in this situation and the women he cared for into whatever man could afford their price.

It was dark when he decided he needed to eat then rest so he could work harder in the morning to rebuild his body. He had made it to the third floor before he ran into a couple of girls going up the stairs.

"Ryan, Mister Westbrook, where have you been? The staff is going crazy looking for you." One of the girls asked him.

"I never left the building, they were just not looking in the right place. So, I guess I best go and let them know I did not run away. Have a nice evening."

He smiled as he moved past them on down the stairway.

When he entered the first floor, there was a group of people gathered in what was once the lobby talking. Jocey broke out of the group and ran to him.

"Ryan, where have you been? We've looked everywhere for you?"

"I was up on the roof, thinking. Right now, I'm going to get something to eat, then go back to my room and relax. If you care to talk, come to the restaurant with me."

He just walked away from her heading for the restaurant never looking back to see if she was following. Once he had a plate of fried chicken and fries, he found a spot in the corner and sat down. Jocey sat down across from him.

"Speak your mind Granddaughter."

"Grandfather you must keep us advised where you are at until we get all of your papers cleaned up. If the inspectors had come to check the clinic and bordello, and had found you without papers, they would have taken you away."

"How much longer before I have my papers?"

"At least another day, maybe two. Why?"

"Jocey, what you, Ciara, and the girls upstairs have to do to live sickens me. Give me a week and I'll be ready to go to work. Find me the targets, and I'll do the rest."

"Ryan, there are other considerations besides just killing."

"Such as?"

Jocey dropped her eyes and Ryan could see her blushing. He commented before she could answer his question.

"My playing a male whore?"

"Only for some powerful female party members who have used our services."

"What's to be gained by that?"

"Access to information otherwise hard to develop. They like to brag about their positions and programs they are responsible for while in bed. Also, once you are known in their circles, you can move about the city without worry from the police. Once you have a pass, such as I have, then you can tackle targets otherwise difficult to approach."

"Does this also mean I would attend parties where you and Ciara will be in attendance?"

"It's possible."

"No. That is a restriction I have to place upon my working in such a manner. Never with you involved because of who you are and not with Ciara."

"You're in love with Ciara, aren't you?"

"Maybe, but if I am, that is not the only reason I need to avoid seeing her with another man."

"I understand Grandfather. I'll let the command staff know of your decision."

"Good. Now I intend to finish this before it gets cold."

Jocey stood up and started to walk away when he spoke again.

"Jocey, pass the word, if I wish company, I'll ask for it, and the only females that can enter my room uninvited is you or Ciara."

"Okay Grandfather, I'll put the word out."

He sat and finished his dinner while thinking about what he had just committed too. This was not how he remembered being in his previous life. He had never been as sexually open and even now he felt as if someone or something was pushing him into such exchanges like a poorly written James Bond parody.

Then his feelings towards those that were forcing him to act as the sheep dog to go after the wolf that was endangering the flock, except the flock itself was soiled. What had happened to him in hibernation to change his basic nature, or had his time in prison then the experiment finally brought out the aggressiveness that even the Marine Corps never brought to the surface?

He had spent his life going along for the ride, just taking care of business without causing ripples whenever possible. Now he was prepared, in his mind, to cause a tidal wave for people he truly did not know and yet, he had this feeling he was being guided into this position by some unknown force, waiting and watching him dance to the music only they could hear.

Whatever it Takes

It was nearly four days before Ciara entered his room, removed her clothes and nearly climbed up his body. For the next two hours it was madness between them as the restrained passion finally released itself. Ciara lay on Ryan as they had finally completed what they both desired and yet, knew it would never be complete under the current circumstances.

"Ryan, I made a terrible mistake with you."

"How so?"

"I never should have entered your mind. I should have brought in another to do the work I did. I did more then sense your growing feelings for me, I embraced them and in doing so, my own feelings are now too strong to ignore as I have tried since we last talked."

"So, what do we do now?"

"I'm conflicted in that I have my responsibilities to the clinic and the children, and yet, I only want you to make love to me."

"Ciara, I understand your dilemma, but until we can find a way to change how things are done, this is the life we both must live. Hour by hour, day by day. I suppose Jocey has talked to you."

"Yes, and I agree with you. But Ryan, Jocey is right. We always gain valuable information during those sessions. And the money helps take care of the kids."

He rolled her off him and came up on an elbow, looking down at her.

"Ciara, I've given this a lot of thought. I may not make it through this but if I do, when I say let's go, pack a bag and come with me."

"Ryan…."

"Please promise me, because then I will have something to hang onto, something to make me fight to return to you."

"Then I promise and not just to make you feel good about what you are doing, but because I will go with you."

For the next two weeks, Ryan pushed himself building muscle and strength. He was running up and down the staircase building his legs and lungs up as he built his torso up. It was a slow process, but he could see definition slowly developing.

He had his papers now and a background to go with them. From time to time he would go out with a street team to see how the world really was outside the hotel. He did not like what he saw. And all the time he was out, he felt he was being watched just as he often felt in the hotel.

When he asked about weapons, Doctor Prescott took him to a room in the basement and after moving several large crates, uncovered a sealed military packing crate. Inside Ryan was pleasantly surprised to find firearms he was familiar with. Another crate held explosives, while a smaller case contained detonators.

Ryan removed a Sig P229 with silencer and spare magazines for his use. Shoulder holster and magazine pouches, plus a long, thin stiletto for close in work. He took everything back to his room and hid it inside an air vent under the desk. He never carried any sort of weapon when out with a street team since the police would arrest him even for a simple pocket knife.

But even without a weapon, he found ways to disrupt work projects. Moving traffic cones causing a police car to drive into a hole in the street the cones was marking off to prevent such accidents. Breaking into a traffic light control box, locking all of the lights on green, causing an accident which blocked the intersection for hours. He wasn't concerned about injuries since very few non-Party members had vehicles and even fewer had fuel ration cards for them.

Ciara only left his bed to fulfill an engagement contract and then would she returned to her own room afterwards to clean the smell of another from her body and to rest. Bryon never spoke of those nights and she never mentioned with who or why she was engaged, and he never took one of the girls from upstairs to his bed on those nights.

Three weeks after Ryan committed to the program, he was asked to attend to a female up on the eighth floor. She was the wife of a senior party member in Denver and had a taste for young girls and a man other than her husband. He was told he would not have to service the girl, but the woman as often as possible. He was not to make any inquiries concerning her position or her husbands, but to let the girl do the talking as she would have experience in such matters.

The girl was eighteen and named Carol. She was a little blond and Ryan had seen her around the hotel with Megan and others. He wasn't happy with the situation, but he had committed himself to what life had handed him to work with.

Carol met him in the eighth-floor hallway and took him to the room they would be using that evening. It had a larger than normal bed and a sparkling white sheet on it. She told him to strip and put on a short robe laying on the bed and he was to stay robed until either the client disrobed him or she herself did. And he was to let her deal with the client at the start since she liked to play with girls before entertaining a man. This was not Carol's first time with this client.

Ryan stripped and put on the robe with Carol smiling at him as she also stripped and put on a like robe. Both robes were colorful satin robes and he just sat on the edge of the bed waiting for the client to arrive.

When the client arrived, she was of modest height and build, wearing clothes suitable for a business meeting. She tossed her purse on a chair looking at Carol then Ryan as she began to undress. Carol removed her robe, moved to her, pulled her head down and they kissed as Carol began to help her undress. Soon she was only wearing nylons and a halter to hold them in place.

The woman moved away from Carol and walked to Ryan as she let her long dark hair down. She stopped close enough to reach the sash holding Ryan's robe closed, opened it and looked down at him and smiled.

"Come here girl, see how hard you can get him."

Ryan knew what the woman was wanting Carol to do and before Carol could get to him he spoke to the woman.

"No, you can get on your knees, and you can taste how large I can get."

The woman laughed and dropped down in front of him. She signaled for Carol to join her as they both were down on him. Once she found out about him, she took Carol to bed as Ryan watched them roll all over it until he found the right time and mounted the woman with her screaming as he entered her.

The night ended with Carol watching him dress nearly three hours later after the woman left walking as if she had a corn cob up her ass. Once the woman was out the door and it was closed behind her, Carol laughed.

"Ryan, she'll be back and probably just for you. If you ever change your mind about a playmate other than Ciara, keep me in mind."

"What was the price for tonight?"

"Two grand. We just paid for five new incubators for the orphanage."

"What else did we gain from this?"

"She's worried about her husband's place on the Party Committee. His projects are not developing as projected and that can cause him to lose his place if they fail."

"Maybe we should insure they fail."

Ryan walked over to the bed and lifted Carol from it. During the session he had kissed her several times and even sucked on her nipples. He kissed her hard before sitting her back on the bed, then he turned for the door as she spoke to him.

"Ryan, what are you going to do when a client wants you to take one of us girls during a session?"

"Do what they are paying for. Carol, I am not of this time. I have to adjust somewhat to this time in history, but I refuse to give up all of my ideals. As enjoyable as it was, I did not do it for the sex, I did it for the clinic and orphanage. If that does not make sense to you don't worry as I am also confused."

Ciara was not in his room when he returned to it which actually made him happy since he did not want to face her after this night. The next morning, he met with Jocey and Doctor Prescott over breakfast and discovered Ciara took a contract last night as he was fulfilling one. Fair was fair, and he just moved on from that.

Ryan asked about that the client he serviced last night. What her husband did and was responsible for. If they derived their power from what they achieved, then why not disrupt their projects, reduce their power?

Find ways to sabotage the projects without making it seem like sabotage. Jocey mentioned the Secret Police for the first time since they had met. They knew where they operated out of, the building, but could never get a clear fix on who they actually were. Ryan told Jocey he would deal with the Secret Police when the time came; but find out all they could about all of the projects they could then find ways to cause problems with them.

Three nights later he serviced the wife of the Chief of Police when she asked for him based upon the word of the woman he and Carol had serviced. She was middle aged and frumpy, but eager to be serviced by someone like Ryan.

Within a week, Ryan was getting calls to service the wives of Party Officials both in the hotel and at their homes. He serviced one wife while the husband sat and watched, then paid him double the contracted price when Ryan left. This bothered Ryan as it seemed no matter the situation, he was able to perform, even more so than in his previous life. Was there something in his programing during hibernation that Ciara either missed, or left for her own enjoyment?

Ryan would often set up on the roof thinking about what he was doing and they information being collected. He could not remember being able to perform as often as he was able to now and wondered, like his enhancement, had something been given him to allow him to perform more often?

And with the information he was receiving, he made suggestions which the street crews took out to people they had working in the alleys and homeless shelters to act upon. Little by little, projects began to fail with the Party members becoming more and more distressed. As that was occurring, the wives were not coming as often as they were trying to save what they could of the money they had been receiving. One project was audited by the Central Party and it was discovered the project manager was skimming money off the project for his own gain.

One side effect was the bordello was not getting the high-end clients they once had, reducing the cash flow to about sixty percent. Ryan had a plan to correct that cash flow problem.

He had learned that there were nearly a dozen bordellos within Denver, but unlike the Hotel, they paid for the privilege to service their clients in kick-backs to the police. When he asked about the clinic paying to stay open, he was told they were exempt because they serviced so many of the Party Members. Again, something did not sound right with that explanation.

Ciara and Ryan had a couple of hours together before he left in the middle of the night to meet with one of the street informants. The informant identified the courier who collected from the other bordellos and the route he would have to take to get the money to Police Headquarters. Ryan sent the informant back to the shelter he was staying at and found the spot he wanted.

Just over an hour later, Ryan put a bullet in the man's head as he was getting into his car after picking up the last extortion payment. Ryan drove the Police Car outside of town, stripped the body and dumped it into a creek before driving further into the country and leaving the car in a wooded area on a road nearly overgrown with weeds and grass.

He disposed of the officer's uniform and equipment in another creek, saving the pistol and magazines for future use if needed. The pack he had brought with him had over seven thousand dollars in it as he made his way back to Denver.

Jogging the twenty miles back into the city was easy, but once inside, he had to be careful of his movements as he moved in the shadows to prevent detection from patrolling police cars. By now the police would know their courier was overdue and would be looking for him. It was nearly daylight when he slipped into the hotel's parking garage, then up the stairs to his room.

He stripped out of his clothes, put his weapons including the additional pistol in his hide along with the pack, then went to wash the night off his body. Ciara joined him in the shower then they took their passion to the bed before he fell asleep.

Ciara was gone when he awoke and went down to eat. He met her in the restaurant as she was working in the clinic with Jocey. The word on the street was the courier had taken off with the money leaving his family behind. Ryan felt bad for the family, but they had to know he was a crooked cop, and his wife had to know he was screwing young girls in several of those bordellos, since that information was widely known on the street. And some of those girls in other bordellos were too young to get a driver's license in Ryan's old life.

That afternoon, inspectors came to the hotel and did a walkthrough of the clinic and the bordello. Two of the men took girls into rooms and used them before they left, telling Doctor Prescott they could not find any deficiencies with either the clinic or the bordello. The two girls were isolated from the others as neither man had undergone pre-sex blood testing for STD's. Twenty-four hours later both girls came back clean and had taken their morning after pill.

Jocey said that was not uncommon for them to do that during an inspection and if they had wanted Ciara or even herself, they would have gone to a room with them because if they didn't, they would find problems and shut them down. Ryan told her that he was familiar with their type.

He never spoke of his next plan.

This Can Get Loud

It was three weeks before the police car was found, but the body and clothes were never discovered. Ryan used that time to wander about the city at odd hours, watching and looking for specific people, especially the Secret Police operatives.

The building those people used as a headquarters was almost laughable as it had very poor security on it. Poor enough that Ryan entered into the basement one night and searched it to locate prime points to set explosives. He even was able to enter their weapons storage room in the basement to find what any Marine would consider a nightmare of neglect.

Two nights later, he again entered the basement and set charges where he felt they would do the best good using remote detonators supplied with the explosives. In the weapons containment area, he placed a charge inside a case of 40mm High Explosive grenades for their grenade launchers. Now all he had to do was get as many operatives inside the building as possible.

The street informants had identified over a dozen of the Secret Police working the streets in various manner of clothing as they were keeping the hope of rebellion squashed with brutal street tactics. Most worked alone and did their work in the shadows, but Ryan had a good fix on who they were and when they worked.

He learned that two operatives used the eighth-floor bordello on a fairly regular basis and always paid for the service. They never used specific girls which would have keyed Ryan to think those girls were working for the Secret Police. They only used the girls that were available at the time.

Ryan also learned other operatives used the other bordellos in town and never paid for that service. When he asked Jocey about that, she said because of who they were, that the men always paid, and were reported to be polite. She suspected it was because so many Party Members used the girls, plus the clinic treated the street walkers for everything from minor scrapes and cuts, to STD's and birth control.

The operatives did ask questions from time to time, but they mostly just came in, did their business and left. But the average girl received two hundred dollars an hour to service a client and the prices went up from there. Either the Secret Police had a fund for such activities, or they were being paid very well for their services.

Ryan's own activities within the bordello had slowed as the Party females were hoarding their money as their own projects or their husband's projects were becoming problematic with sabotage by day workers, or his own nighttime activities, plus the audits making them keep the money handy in an attempt to hold off any accusations of graft.

The first female he had serviced returned three times just for him alone. Her name was Linda and between couplings, she was very talkative without much prodding. Her husband's projects were in trouble while her own were also facing problems she could not understand. Her husband also had a mistress who was pregnant.

Ryan treated her like a whore which she seemed to enjoy using her how he wanted and in ways he would never treat another woman just to get her reactions. She never complained and accepted him in the manner he put her in. He learned she was from one of the original families that caused the change in political atmosphere in the country and her husband was a minor player when they first met. Linda suspected he only courted her to gain influence within the party.

He held no sympathy for Linda as she chose the life she was living. A life of false power over others that he intended to bring down around her. And tonight, after he had expended himself as far as humanly possible, he was going to make the first strike in bringing down that system.

After she left, he took a long shower and changed into his street clothes, looking like one of the homeless street people. The clothing was tattered but without the normal odor of sweat and dirt found on the homeless. He did not want his targets smelling him this night.

He took out the first Secret Police operative after the operative came out of a bordello. The kill was quick and clean as Ryan drove his thin stiletto into the back of his neck and up into the brain, killing him instantly.

Ryan drug the body back into an alley and stripped him of everything he could find, then left the body under a pile of debris. Two blocks later, he tossed everything except for the money into a dumpster as he moved to locate his next target. He was tempted to keep the handgun the operative was carrying, but he was risking enough with the stiletto if stopped and questioned by the police.

He took out five more operatives before he moved to his hide position where he could watch the Secret Police Headquarters. In the hide was his pack with his silenced handgun and the remote detonator. Ryan figured leaving the last three bodies where they could be found would cause the Police Headquarters to fill with operatives wanting to know what happened and to get their orders. He was not wrong.

Men and women began pouring into the Headquarters in all manner of dress soon after daylight. Ryan watched as they went in and no one was leaving the building. Several City Police Cars showed up with the officers entering the building including the Chief of Police. Ryan smiled at the thought his wife would be looking for a new lover soon.

Two nights before, Ryan had entered the basement and sealed a small utility room near the center of the building. Inside the room he had two, twenty-pound propane bottles he had earlier brought in and he once he felt he had the room sealed well enough with silicone foam he had stolen off a construction site, he opened the valves on the propane bottles, then closed and sealed the door. Inside with the leaking propane was a quarter pound charge of C-4.

Ryan watched as fewer people reported to the Headquarters and felt if he waited much longer, they would start back out onto the street. His only concern now was that the detonators worked as designed. As tempting as it was to watch, he ducked behind some HVAC equipment on the roof of the building he was on and pushed the detonate command button on the remote. He was rewarded with the sound of the building basically imploding from the blast of the charges throughout the basement.

Some debris came down on the roof he was on but the way he was positioned, it barely missed him. He looked up over his protective barrier to see a large fireball rising up and smile knowing that the propane had done its job. Moving to the edge of the roof, he saw the four-story building had collapsed on itself and down into the basement, leaving a pile of rubble about a single story high. Anyone within the building were either dead or dying. Cars outside the building were overturned and tossed all over the street that he could see from his position. Ryan picked his things up and left his hide for what was now his home in the hotel.

He entered the hotel via the parking garage and stashed his pack for later retrieval as he did not want anyone in the hotel to see him carrying it. The activity in the lobby and clinic was chaos as people were running around talking about the explosion eight blocks away. Vehicles of all sorts were bringing in victims to the clinic that had been caught in the debris field of the blast. Ryan hated that aspect of what he had done, but he could not do anything about that and just took to the stairs to his room.

Ciara, knowing he had a contract the night before would have spent the night in her room to give him a chance to relax and recover as she did when she took a contract. By doing so, she would not know he had been out all night. He showered and went to bed thinking what his next move would be.

He was awakened by Ciara just after noon as she came in with her white lab coat splattered with blood. He joined her in the shower and then made long, slow love until she fell asleep in his arms. Later as they were getting dressed to go eat, she posed a possible contract for him.

"Ryan, I have a client. A female client that has heard about you and desires a threesome with me being the third. She's in her late fifties, in good physical shape and is a generous lover, both in bed and the pocketbook. She said she would double the going rate if you would join us."

"How often do you see her?"

"On the average, twice a month. She's a widow and claims she has not had a man since her husband was killed in a plane crash several years ago. I made her no promises, only that I would talk to you. I did invite her to come here and let you service her alone, but her Party standing is one which it would not be good for her to be seen coming to a bordello."

"Okay, now give me the rest?"

"She's been a good source of information, just bits and pieces but it has all been good information. But now we are starting to feel the cash flow problem from upstairs. Income is down over a third since we started sabotaging the projects in the area. Even with what you brought in from the crooked cops, we need more money coming in. This will help."

"Ciara, tell me what you really want."

"Ryan, I want to get away from all of this. To run away with you and have children and try to lead as normal a life as possible. I'll leave right now if you want, but what about the children we leave behind?"

There were tears in Ciara's eyes as she spoke. Ryan stepped over to her, took her in his arms and just held her.

"It's going to get worse around here baby, but do you want our children raised where political position determines their legacy?"

"No, and you know that."

"Are you going to be okay with me having sex with another woman with you in the same bed?"

"No, but we need the money. Remember when you were told that doing these things would open doors for you? This is the main gate to it all. If she lets it known that you have serviced her, no one would dare to interfere with you as you move around, even after you killing all those people this morning."

"What do you mean this morning?"

"Oh God Ryan, how naïve do you think I am? The reports we were hearing in the clinic was that it was a gas explosion that brought down the Secret Police Headquarters. But to have that happen when nearly all their operatives were in the building plus the Chief of Police and his Lieutenants was just karma? No, you did that and right now, they are wide open, but we need more intelligence on how to take advantage of it."

"Alright then, when do we do this? With this lady client of yours."

"I'll contact her, let her know tonight is out of the question so you have time to rest more."

"I could use some more rest and that also goes for you too. No contracts until we do this."

"Okay Ryan."

Inside Out

Three nights later, Ryan and Ciara were picked up by a Police Car and taken to what was a mansion on the southern edge of Denver. They were let out at the door and the car drove away leaving them on the sidewalk. Ciara told Ryan earlier that was how she always arrived here and later returned to the hotel.

Ciara rang the doorbell and a few moments later an attractive woman opened the door and smiled at them. Ciara stepped in and kissed the woman for a long time before breaking the kiss then stepping aside.

"Margie, this is Ryan. Ryan, Margie, our client."

Ryan stepped into the house, took Margie's face in both hands and gave her a long kiss feeling Margie's tongue flick across his lips. He broke the kiss and stepped back.

"My pleasure Margie."

"Damn Ryan, if you are as good as that kiss, then tonight is going to be fun for sure. Please, let's go where we can get comfortable and see what the night brings."

Margie wrapped her arm around Ciara's waist as they walked through the mansion towards the back of the house. Ryan watched as Margie's hand moved down to Ciara's ass and squeezed it. He smiled as he followed watching Ciara return the grasp on Margie's ass. Yes, he thought, this might be fun after all.

When they entered a room at the rear of the house, Margie stood aside as they entered then closed and locked the door behind them. The room was large, almost a house within itself, with a large bed off to one side. There was a table with bottles of champagne and plates of what appeared to be sliced fruit. The furniture in the room was ornate, almost delicate looking, with two couches long enough to make love on.

Ryan looked back at Margie to witness her dress falling off her nude body to the floor. He smiled as he looked at Ciara to see she had taken her dress off as she smiled at him. He pulled his shirt out of his pants and began to unbutton it as Margie stepped to him.

"You can remove your shirt, but those trousers belong to me. Come, a bit of champagne before we get too excited."

She walked to the table and poured three glasses of champagne as Ryan removed his shirt while following her. She handed Ciara a glass, then Ryan before picking up her own. As she sipped on her glass, she ran her hand over Ryan's smooth, muscular chest.

Margie took his hand and guided him to a couch and invited him to sit down. She placed her glass on the coffee table then leaned over and kissed him, working her tongue into his mouth. As she was doing that she was opening his trousers. Ryan felt Ciara remove his shoes as Margie was opening his trousers, then reaching her hand in to find what she was paying for tonight. Ryan wasn't wearing underwear tonight and Margie had no problem finding him.

For over an hour they played on the couch with Margie and Ciara servicing him with their mouths then Margie sitting on the couch as Ciara serviced her while Margie and Ryan kissed, or he took her breasts with his mouth.

Margie took Ciara to bed and made love to her as Ryan made love to Ciara's breasts until Margie moved around into the sixty-nine position. After a few minutes of this play, Ryan lifted Margie above Ciara and took her in that position for a long time with Margie almost screaming as he used her.

Ryan took his time with Margie, changing positions, often allowing Ciara to service her while he relaxed, prolonging his first climax while drawing multiple climaxes from Margie. He finally took her from behind as she and Ciara were in a sideways sixty-nine position and she was screaming and shaking as he filled her with his ejaculation.

Margie was laying on his chest after his second go at her shaking and covered in sweat with Ciara lying on his other side. He was worn out and hoping that she did not want another go with him. Margie leaned over and kissed Ciara, then went down on him, cleaning him of her own juices before she got up and went to the table, pouring a glass of champagne and nibbling on a piece of fruit.

Ciara just snuggled in closer and softly kissed him. He knew from the sounds Ciara made during the portions of the sessions between her and Margie that she had climaxed several times. Margie filled a second glass and walked back to the bed, or actually slightly limped to bed, carefully crawled up on it and straddled Ryan's waist, sitting on his flaccid manhood.

She carefully poured a bit of champagne in Ryan's mouth then offered some to Ciara. Margie took a long drink of her glass, emptying it, then smile at Ryan.

"My daughter was right, you are one hell of a lover. Too bad she is otherwise an idiot."

"Who are you talking about Margie?" Ryan asked.

"Linda. I think she married that jackass to spite me. But the night is still young, so Mister Bryon Petersen, why don't you tell me your next move against the Party?"

"Who is Bryon Peterson?" Ryan responded to her comment.

"You are dear. Jimmy did a wonderful job changing your appearance. I like this look better than your Petersen ID or even your Reynolds look."

Ryan was unsure what to do as Ciara slowly moved off him, freeing up his right arm. Margie continued without waiting for another response from him.

"Ryan, Jim Prescott is my nephew by my older sister. I saw how fouled up the Socialist system was while Ciara was waiting to get her first period and you were a popsicle. I funded the orphanage, so Jim could be near to do what had to be done. When I learned that you were going to be thawed out, I did a bit of research and discovered Jocey. I had her brought to Denver for the very purpose of getting you away from the bastards that are ruining this country."

She emptied her second glass before continuing.

"Ciara, I paid for your education because you were too intelligent to just be a whore. If Ryan can break the back of the Party, people like you will be needed to help the public return to self-sufficiency."

"Yet you let Ciara and Jocey sell their bodies to fund the orphanage. Why?" Ryan asked.

"Because if I continued to fund the orphanage, and the clinic, it would be discovered, and my usefulness would be lost. This room is sound proof and if there was a listening device in it, an alarm would have sounded the moment it was activated. But that's not the only secret this house actually holds."

She climbed off him and stood by the bed.

"Come with me. I think you will appreciate what I am going to show you."

Margie walked over to the bookcase behind the champagne table and reached into it and a section of shelves moved backwards then swung open, revealing an opening. She reached into the opening and flipped a switch. Ryan was holding Ciara's hand as they moved to the opening and saw it was a staircase. Margie started down the stairs.

Ryan stepped in front of Ciara and followed Margie down the steps. If this was a trap, it was very convoluted to say the least as Margie knew all about him and could have had him removed at any time since he arrived in Denver. He was still puzzled by several things, but he could wait for those answers another time. At the bottom of the steps, Margie flipped another light switch, illuminating the basement.

When Ryan was at a point he could look well into the basement, he froze. He could not believe what he was seeing laid out before him. Ryan moved on down the steps to the bottom where Margie was waiting and looked around. The basement was massive, and it had racks of M-4 Infantry Rifles, waiting for someone to take them out and use them.

He walked to the tables with pistols in display racks. Another table held stacks of magazines for the rifles while another table had stacks of magazines for the pistols. No matter where he looked were weapons and their components. Looking back towards the stairs the room expanded, with stacks of small wooden crates, each containing two ammunition boxes of small arms ammunition, that without closely examining each crate he had no idea if it was for the rifles or pistols, or both.

Margie walked up to him, pulled his head down and kissed him hard as she handled his manhood. When she broke the kiss, she held onto him as she spoke.

"My father put this down here in case the Socialist Revolution needed weapons of war, but war came to this country and politics did the rest. This is all yours to do with as you feel you need to fix what my father broke, and my husband crippled. My husband never knew about this section of the basement, but now you do."

"Margie, you could have shown me this without all the sex games. So why?"

"Why the sex games? Because I have honestly missed having a man make love to me. No, you were not making love to me as much as you were just fucking me, but I have missed that part of me. I just figured after Linda told me about you, I would enjoy you too. Call all of this a bonus above the agreed fee."

Ryan looked at Ciara who had a stunned look on her face as she viewed the weapons.

"Margie, how do you want to play this?" He asked her.

"When you leave here tomorrow, you will take a panel truck, a van I have in the garage area. It has my personal plates on it, so it is immune from being stopped and searched as long as you don't do something stupid while driving. It's yours along with one of my fuel ration cards. Take what you want and return when you need more items from here. And Ciara is welcome to return with you so maybe I can enjoy this more, or just her while you are gathering what you need."

"What happens to you if I succeed in bringing down the Party?"

"Not much really. I have enough cash on hand to deal with that end of it. No matter what happens, there will still be the need for currency until a new government can be formed and issue new money, plus I have gold and silver locked away if needed. Party records will show I have never had any direct influence and very little indirect influence on the Party's actions, so basically, I'm a neutral. My power comes from being my father's daughter, and the widow of a powerful Party leader."

Ciara walked over to them, pulled Margie's face over and kissed her, then pulled Ryan over and kissed him. Ryan had the feeling as he often had in that he was being manipulated and there was absolutely nothing he could do about it. He gently removed

Margie's hand from his manhood and walked back to the stairs, looked back at the women, then started up the stairs.

An hour later he took Margie again then proclaimed he was spent. He got up from the bed, took a shower then only putting on his pants and shoes, he went back down into the basement and began a mental inventory of the assets he had been given. Ryan estimated he could outfit a short battalion with what he found available to him, but where would he find the people capable of being trained and where to train them?

He went back upstairs to find the women entwined as they slept. He stripped and gently moved in behind Ciara, snuggling in close to her and went to sleep. The next morning, he was awakened by the sounds of the women enjoying each other and he just moved to the edge of the bed to give them plenty of room as he knew he was not capable of joining them.

Once they were satisfied, Margie got up and moaned as she did, saying she had not been that sore since the night she lost her virginity. She made a pot of coffee in the small kitchenette in her apartment, then took Ciara to the shower to cleanse themselves of the nights activities.

Margie produced a tray of pastries made just before they arrived the night before and they sat sipping on the coffee and eating pastries and fruit as they talked. Neither female had dressed, and Ryan only had his pants on during this time. Margie tried to explain the best she could her vision of a new country which Ryan felt was what he had left so many years ago.

"Margie, if the government is in Sacramento, why am I wasting my time here in Denver?"

"Sacramento is only the capital in the public eyes. The original revolution started here in Denver and this is where the true Party Committee meets. Denver is the government behind the government. What the Party Committee decides, the Party

111

Congress decrees. The Central Committee is spread all over the country but meets yearly here in Denver to determine the next years path. You have four months to further weaken Denver before they meet. And if you make enough noise, they will meet before then."

"The street people, the day workers are doing a good job of disrupting projects in Denver at the risk to themselves in both injury and loosing income and food. How do we contain that problem?"

"You find a half-dozen locations and I'll arrange soup kitchens to supplement the shelters. This will employ some and feed many more. What funds the Party here does not have, I can get from the Central Committee."

"You make that sound simple Margie."

"Well, I do sit on the Committee, so yes, it is simple. I fill my father's and husband's seat now. I have to play the game with them, but as brilliant as some of the Committee members are, they are blinded by their own image of utopia, even as they travel through the stench of their own failures."

"That's all well and good, but we are sitting on top enough equipment to outfit a short battalion, but where do I find the men, then a place to train them?"

"In two months I'll have the men for you. Men who you will be able to train and trust. The hatred for the Socialist government runs deep and the men will be available. Where to train them has taken time to develop. I have a large area outside of Aspin that the Committee has determined to be a preserve and is now isolated from the rest of the country, so no one will bother you there. It took some doing on my part, but the Greens within the party are easily convinced when you make a plea to save some silly worm or beetle from extinction."

"You've given this a lot of thought, haven't you?"

"Yes, I have Ryan. I've had years to think and plan this. Now either you remove your trousers and let's see if you can work some of this soreness out of me, or we need to figure out what you want to take with you from the basement when you leave."

"Margie, my groin aches from your abuse of it last night, so maybe another time."

Margie laughed, got up and went over to Ryan, straddled him and kissed him hard.

"Anytime, just knock on the door and I'll spread wide for you." She looked over at Ciara. "Ciara, you are one lucky lady. I think I'm jealous of both of you."

Margie got off Ryan and stepped over to Ciara and kissed her.

"I guess we had better get dressed and help Ryan load the van." She moved her hips a couple times. "Ryan, I think another go with you this morning may not have been the right idea. Damn, my hips ache too."

She laughed as she went to get dressed. Ciara moved to Ryan, kissed him before she got up to get dressed. All Ryan could do was watch them as he finished dressing.

Once dressed, Margie went to her desk and removed two envelopes and handed them to Ryan. One contained the money for the night and the other contained identification for him showing him as an employee of hers and the permit for the van.

"How did you arrange the ID?"

"Where do you think Jim got your ID from in the first place? He knew I was going to expose him to you but try not to put him in an embarrassing position. In a way I'm the inside man to the Committee and he is the outside man to the Resistance. And one last thing Ryan. No more blowing up buildings without letting me know first. I lost a good agent in that blast. Collateral damage

113

of course and you could not have known about him, but no more rouge operations, understand?"

"Margie, if you are going to control what I do then call the police and have me arrested now."

"No Ryan, you misunderstood what I meant. Give me a warning so if I need to get one or more of my people out of harm's way, if I can. Also, if I can find a way to help, I will, to include having my people assist you. It's taken years to glean out the people I have working for me. They might work in the system, but they hate it as much as I do. Trust is a hard thing to develop, but I do trust the ones I have on my personal payroll."

"Alright, let's go load up my van."

As they drove back to the hotel, Ryan thought about the mansion and the arms beneath it. The only way anyone could afford to build such a house and stock it with millions of dollars' worth of weapons and equipment was through capitalism. But to support socialism was a contradiction except for one aspect of greed even Marx missed. The greed for power above what they had already at hand. To use one to support the other, and the so-called projects he had been sabotaging were capitalistic in nature, except ran by socialists for their own power over those working for them.

It was a weak concept in his mind, but one that fit the situation as he saw it.

Timing

Four days after meeting Margie, Ciara turned thirty, and a small party was held in the clinic's restaurant with cake and punch. Ciara and Ryan slipped away during the party to celebrate in his room with a bottle of champagne he had brought from Margie's just for this occasion.

As they slept, exhausted from their coupling, one of the clothing factories in Denver burnt to the ground due to faulty wiring. Everyone escaped unharmed, but the building and machinery was a total loss. The next morning, Margie opened her first soup kitchen in that area to help compensate for the loss of income and the ability to purchase food by the now, out of work employees.

Ciara worked in the clinic that morning as Ryan drove around looking for his next target and places for Margie's soup kitchens. While he was out, Linda called the bordello's appointments desk to arrange for another night with Ryan. She was told he was booked up for the next two weeks even though he did not have a single appointment scheduled. Ciara's schedule was also shown to be booked for that same time frame.

Ryan moved about at night, mostly walking the streets, watching, observing the movements of the street walkers and drug dealers. Four members of a street gang tried to mug him late one night, but he left one dead, and two badly injured with the fourth running as fast as he could away from the scene. Ryan just slipped through several alley's until he was far from the scene then made his way back to the hotel to remove his bloody clothes from the incident. He was unhurt, but the bloody clothes gave away his actions.

Between what he had learned in the Marines plus the knowledge fed him about Ranger training, hand to hand combat came easy to him.   It also scared him some that he had that knowledge.

Another night he damaged several pieces of heavy equipment at a building site, bypassing the less than attentive security guard.   He rendered them inoperable by pouring dry cement into the fuel tanks of the equipment.

It was a week after he had driven the van from Margie's to the hotel, he was refueling it early one morning when he received a message from Margie.   A police officer pulled into the refueling station and positioned his car close enough to speak to Ryan from his rolled, down window.

"Are you Ryan?"

"Yes Officer, can I help you?"

"Margie wants to see you."

"Thanks."   Ryan replied as the officer was driving off.

Ryan drove out to the mansion considering two things. First, she had information for him and the second was that she would want him to service her.   Ciara had told Ryan she understood that if he had to go out to see Margie, that aspect of the relationship was just something he had to do and deal with on his own.   Ryan felt that in a sense, he was bought and paid for because all she had to do was pick up a phone and he was a dead man without trial.

Margie met him at the door and never made a move on him as she led him back to her apartment in the mansion.   She handled him a three-ring binder off her desk, along with a thick envelope.

"Ryan, here is a break-down of all of the projects in the area.   This will give you a much better feel for what is happening and how to deal with some of them than just moving around as you have been doing.   Also, there is ten thousand dollars in that envelope. Half is for the clinic; the other half is for your expenses needing cash while you work. I hope this helps."

He was thumbing through the printed pages.

"Thanks, this will help a lot. Is there anything else?"

She went to her knees.

"Yes, we don't have time for anything else, but I never did get a chance the other night to do more than get you hard. Come here."

Ryan met Ciara for lunch and told her about being called out to Margie's. Ciara looked over her cup as he just told here about picking up the folder.

"Anything else Ryan?"

"She blew me, that's all. Damn, I hate this situation Ciara. This is the most confounding mess I could ever dream of, and I hate it."

"I hate it too Ryan. I used to be able to take a man without thought, just lay back and enjoy it, but now, I have to focus, close part of my mind to what I am doing to keep from getting sick in my stomach. I like Margie, but still, the thought of her having you, especially since you cannot refuse to service her makes me want to ball up and cry."

"I feel the same way with you, baby. But what are we going to do? You're right, we just can't leave, not now, with Margie knowing who I really am."

"There is one thing you, or we can do Ryan, if you want?"

"What's that?"

"Get me pregnant. That will take me off the availability list, and I won't have to service anyone. Just work here in the clinic."

117

"Is that what you want? If I fail, if someone gets lucky and takes me out of your life, do you want to raise a child in this environment?"

"I've talked to Jocey about it, and we both agree that it is a risk. But if something does happen to you, then I'll have a part of you to hold and remember you by."

Ryan sat for a long time thinking about the situation and the position Ciara being pregnant would put her in.

"So, I guess we are getting married?"

"No Ryan, we are not. Getting pregnant is one thing, married is another. If we get married, the entire hotel will know about it, then soon the street will know about it, and then I can become a target to be used against you. Getting pregnant only tells people we made a mistake, and my anti-abortion feelings are well known here."

"It's a big step to take, honey?"

"I know, but it's one I'm willing to take. Give me a baby."

"What do we have to do, I mean other than just enjoy each other?"

"I have to have my implant removed then there is a shot I have to take to neutralize the effects of the implant. I'll have flu like symptoms for a couple of days then from that point on, nature takes over. Jocey has already told me she can remove the implant anytime I want. But I have callers wanting me right now, and I can only put them off for so long in my current condition."

He thought for a moment, remembering his feelings about not seeing his son Jacob grow up, or holding Jocey as a baby and he felt the loss of those memories he never had available to him. He had mixed feelings about Ciara's request, but would give in to her.

118

"Damn, this is rushing things, but alright, I'll give you what you want."

"Thank you. I'll have Jocey remove the implant this afternoon and take the shot. You deal with Margie and any others as you see fit. Hopefully by the time the child is born, we will be free of this mess."

That afternoon, Ryan was sitting in his room, studying the information Margie had given him when Ciara came in and sat down on the edge of the bed and began taking her shoes off.

"Honey, this is not an invitation. My stomach is all messed up and I feel as if I've been run over by a truck. Either I'm more sensitive to the shot or Jocey misread the chart and gave me too much because I feel like shit."

Ryan moved to help her undress.

"Did you tell Jocey about how you feel?"

"Yeah, she said she would come up in about an hour to check on me. Sorry dear, but no fun and games tonight."

Ryan tucked her in, gave her a kiss on her forehead, feeling the heat coming off her body as if she had a bad fever. This concerned him and once she was curled up under a sheet he went down to see Jocey. Jocey told him that she had double checked the dosage on the charts and in the syringe before giving Ciara the shot. She told him she thought the manufacture did not properly process and test the drug prior to shipment and the date on the vial shows it to be less than a third into its shelf life.

When Ryan returned to his room, he found Carol sitting on the sofa, reading a book. She looked up and smiled a knowing smile, then went back to her book. Ryan moved close, so he could lower his voice to talk to her.

"Carol, what are you doing here?"

"Doctor Prescott called upstairs wanting someone to sit with Ciara while you went out, so I volunteered."

"That's nice of you, but I'm not sure when or even if I'm going out tonight."

"Well if I'm down here, that means I'm not up there waiting for some jerk with a small penis to pound on me then proclaim himself to be the world's greatest lover. If you do not mind, I'll just sit here and read. You do what you have to do, alright?"

Ryan bent over and gave her a quick peck on the lips.

"Thanks Carol, you being here will take a lot of worry off me."

She just winked at him and went back to reading.

Ryan found his next target in the folder, told Carol he would be back when he got back, then left. He was going to give a brewery a major problem. He drove around the brewery once, getting a feel for the area and looking for the water and gas mains for the plant.

He first turned the water off, insuring that there would be no water entering the facility to supply the vats brewing the beer. As he understood it, the vats were being heated and water was added as needed during the process, so they could achieve the proper blend. No water, the blend became too thick and even develop a burned taste, souring the mix.

Ryan traced the water main to the brewery finding two more mains, leaving the nearest one alone, but turning off the next one. This would cause plant maintenance valuable time in locating the problem and turning the water back on.

He continued to move around the city, stopping from time to time to check on the soup kitchens Margie was establishing so if she asked him about them, he could give her his view point. He also checked on two homeless shelters which Margie sponsored to see if they had everything they needed, which the common reply was no, they could make do with what they had.

When he returned to the hotel, it was nearing midnight and he found Carol laid out on the couch asleep. Her pull-over smock had risen up exposing her pubis to him and for a moment, he remembered the night they serviced Linda. He covered her up with a sheet, took a short shower and laid down with Ciara. Ciara's body was hot from her fever, so he put a pillow between them and went to sleep.

During the night he heard Ciara weakly call out and as he rolled over to check on her, he saw Carol helping Ciara out of bed, then assist her to the bathroom. He got up to see if he could help but it looked like Carol had everything under control. Ryan just stood back and was ready to help if needed. It wasn't until Carol helped Ciara back to bed and looked down at his groin that he realized he was not wearing underwear. She grinned at him as she helped Ciara back in bed. Once Ciara was tucked back in, Carol blew Ryan a kiss, then went back to the couch, this time insuring she was covered up. Ryan laid back down and went to sleep since it was too late to put underwear on now, but he would have to watch that later on. Then he remembered she had not only seen him erect and involved with Linda, she had assisted Linda in getting him erect during the evening, so she knew how he really was in and out of bed.

For three days, Carol took care of Ciara, only leaving the room to get a fresh smock or a different book. Meals were being brought up on a schedule, so they would not have to leave Ciara alone, and Carol often helped Ciara with the plain broth soup she was being fed.

Ryan had gone out one night and during his walks amongst the homeless, he killed two drug dealers, emptying their pockets of everything they had and dumping it all into the sewers except for the money which he kept for the clinic. The bodies were covered with trash and debris in alleys which meant it would take days before anyone found them.

On the fourth day, Ciara was sitting up, her fever had broken but she was weak. Carol had gone to her room to change her smock and Ryan was spooning chicken soup into Ciara.

"Ryan, will you do something for me?"

"If I can."

"When Carol returns, take her to my room and put a smile on her face. She's been bathing me, wiping my nasty ass and elsewhere. She told me that the night that you and her met with Linda, you barely touched her. I'll be alright here alone now, so take her and give her a couple of hours and make it count."

"So, payment by penis?"

"Well since I can't do anything to put a smile on your face, why not? Yes, my love, this is a screwed-up world we live in, but we are living in a bordello, and I understand she is very good I bed."

"Alright I will for you, but only this once. But since you are now no longer servicing men, why don't you take Carol to bed once you are back on your feet?"

Ciara smiled. "I intend too. But for now, you take care of her." Ciara pulled his head to hers and kissed him. "That's the best I have for now."

It was nearly midnight when Ryan returned to his room, showered and crawled into bed to find Ciara's body warm, but not too hot to snuggle up to. She spoke as he settled in.

"So, is she happy now?"

"Damn that girl is insatiable. But she is asleep on your bed with a large smile on her face. But I may not walk normal for a couple of days though."

Ciara lightly laughed.

"Go to sleep my love. You'll feel better in the morning."

Carol woke them the next morning when she brought the breakfast cart into the room. She never spoke about the previous evening and Ryan figured wearing underwear in her presence was a waste of time. Carol stayed with Ciara for two more days, helping her as she was weak from the fever. Ryan entered his room on Carol's last day helping Ciara to find a note on his desk from Ciara telling him they were in her room and to fend for himself.

Three days later Ryan was putting his trousers on as Margie watched from her bed. She had given him a report on how his activities were disrupting the Party and two envelopes containing a total of twenty thousand dollars. Her idea was to spread the money around to the street people anyway he felt best. Ryan never commented that one hundred-dollar bills was difficult to spread around without raising a lot of unnecessary questions.

Margie told him that the people she had for him to train were starting to gather near Aspin and asked when he would be ready to start training them. He told her when there were at least fifty people on site, he would go to Aspin, otherwise, they were on their own until then. He understood they were being sheltered and fed but had no weapons or anyone in charge. Privately he was hoping the strong would step forward and lead before he got there.

Back at the hotel, he sat down with Doctor Prescott, gave him five thousand dollars for the clinic, then another twelve thousand to find a way to break it down into more manageable bills to spread around. Later that night he made love to Ciara.

It was three weeks after Ciara recovered from her fever that she was pronounced pregnant. It was both a joyful and sad occasion as Ryan received a message to head for Aspin. Ryan was also informed that weapons and equipment were ready for him to pick up at the mansion by himself as Margie was holding that secret as close to her breasts as possible.

This time everything would be loaded into one of Margie's box-bed farm trucks since there was more than the van would hold. It took him five hours to load the van by himself, then Margie sat him on her couch and first orally induced him then rode him until he was empty.

Ryan admitted later to himself that if he had not been working out almost daily, the loading and her sexual assault on him would have incapacitated him. He arrived at the camp just after dark and the people there showed him where his small hut was, so he could rest before starting training the next day.

Timing was everything. Ciara was expecting, Carol said she would stay with Ciara to insure she was never alone. Margie was telling him events were moving as she predicted and now he had to get men ready in less than sixty days to start a revolution.

In the back of his mind, he wondered what Margie's actual goal was in all of this?

Aspin Camp

Ryan stood in the early morning light sipping on a cup of coffee looking at the camp he now was in charge of. There were ten barracks buildings capable of holding twenty men per building with a shower and toilet facilities. Between the fifth and sixth barrack buildings was a dining hall capable of holding two hundred with a kitchen in the back.

He quickly learned the people operating the kitchen were not part of his trainees, but people hired by Margie to feed his troops. According to what Margie had told him, the camp was built with funds directed for a youth camp. Ryan was beginning to become concerned that there might be too many people involved in this secret, which meant trouble.

As he was trying to come to grips with this new task, a man who seemed to be in his mid-thirties came walking across the open ground to him. He stopped a few feet away from Ryan and nodded.

"Major Westbrook, my name is Jasper Hanna, and I guess I am in charge of this gaggle of geese. At least they voted me in as in charge. Sorry if I didn't salute but no one is sure what the protocol will be here."

"Mister Hanna, no saluting period. Now why don't we get the people in some sort of formation and get the show on the road."

"Yes Sir."

Hanna turned towards the buildings and whistled real loud then yelled out for a formation. Almost immediately men came running out of the barracks and fell into a rough formation in front of him. Ryan sat his coffee cup down and stepped off the small porch he had been standing on.

"Gentlemen, raise your hands if you have any military or police experience."

Everyone raised their hands.

"Alright, put them down. This will make our time here easier. Now, my name is Westbrook and I'm the final word here. I see everyone is dressed in a uniform, so this also make some things easier. Since you have voted that Mister Hanna is in charge, he is now Captain Hanna."

He paused for a second.

"I'm not going to give some grand lecture on the evils of socialism, or the corruption eating away at this country. If you were not already aware of it, you would not be here today. So here is what is going to happen this morning. In the back of that box truck are weapons and equipment. When you fall out, get that truck empty, sort out the gear and every man get outfitted. Captain Hanna, I want the ammunition crates stacked beside my porch, unopened. Get this done then we'll work on learning how to use those weapons since they are before your time."

"Captain Hanna, fall the men out and execute your orders."

Ryan stepped back to his cup, picked it up and went back inside his hut to refill it. He could hear Hanna barking orders and then others echoing them as they went to work. He went back and sat down on the porch and watched as the men went to work.

It took a little more than an hour for the men to get the gear sorted out and each man to get themselves outfitted to include weapons. Hanna came over to him and told Ryan that the rifles were very similar to the ones used by the military today, so learning them would be easy.

Once outfitted, Ryan told Hanna to form the men into thirteen men squads. A squad leader and three, four-man teams. Hanna told him that they had already selected Lieutenants which made that part easy on Ryan. As the men were forming into teams and squads, Ryan asked Hanna his own background. Hanna had served in the Army then as a police officer. He was forced out of

126

the police department in Wichita because he would not become a party member.

Later that afternoon, Ryan sat down with Hanna and the units Lieutenants to lay out a training program based on what they told him about the men under his command. Before he entered the experiment, he would have never considered training even a squad, but the knowledge he had been given proved beneficial in this endeavor. Primary training was to ensure each man was qualified with the weapons at hand, then small team training in taking buildings and rooms, utilizing the barracks as those training facilities.

For the next three days, Ryan ran every man through marksmanship qualification to determine how much work they would need before sending them out to do the real thing. He was surprised how well the shot and maintained their weapons. Ryan zeroed his own rifle then shot with the entire company watching. His skill with the rifle then later with the pistol impressed the men he was to lead.

Ryan visited with the men when he could to get a sense of them, how they thought and what they thought about overthrowing the current government. He still had mixed feelings about what was going to happen, especially with a group of unknowns. Who in this group were infiltrators, and who reported back to Margie?

Ten days after his arrival, he told Hanna to keep the men working on team tactics while he went back to Denver to retrieve more ammunition and other things they needed.

Ryan pulled into the parking garage of the hotel at daylight and took the elevator to his floor. When he walked into the room he found Ciara and Carol wrapped up with each other with no covers on their bodies. He stripped then woke them both by tickling their feet before joining them in a mass of flesh moving over the bed as he serviced both women before he just lay back, exhausted from the experience.

127

He later told Ciara if she was going to sleep with Carol on his bed, then he was going to enjoy her too since they were not married. Ciara laughed then kissed him before he got out of bed and showered. He still had things to do, and time was short.

It was late in the afternoon by the time Ryan had more ammunition loaded onto the truck. Margie wanted him to spend the night with her, but he said he had to get back. She took him from behind, lying over the padded arm of a couch before he left.

Ryan never asked her if she had informants in the company but figured she would lie to him if she did. He had another plan in mind for the men, one she would not suspect.

He observed the training the next day and decided that without hard, urban combat training, this was going to get as good as it could get. The men had been trained in riot control in the military and small unit tactics so there wasn't much he had to do except point them at a target.

Ryan honestly did not know what two hundred and eight men could do to turn a country around, but he was obligated to try with what he had.

That night he returned to Denver with the first load of men and equipment. Twenty men with their gear and cots made for a bit crowded ride but it was the only way he could get them into the city without a hassle. Once in the underground parking garage, he told the men to spread out and stay hidden as well as possible until he came back for them. Ryan then went to find Doctor Prescott.

He told Prescott he was going to place the men on the sixth floor, four men to a room and they had brought cots to sleep on. Ryan told Prescott not to inform his aunt about the men being in the city as he had doubts about her sincerity in this endeavor. Prescott did not react as Ryan feared as he told Ryan he also had more questions than answers why she was doing what she had been doing.

Ryan told Prescott he would try to divert rations for the men, so they would not take way from the orphans. Prescott told Ryan all he had to do was ask for more rations and Margie would see they had them. She had never questioned the need for food for the kids or the girls upstairs.

By the time Ryan had all of the men in the hotel, occupying the sixth floor and part of the eighth, he was tired, especially since he had gone back to the mansion several times picking up more equipment such as radios and even hand grenades. Margie even gave him the payroll for the men after she had him on her bed for nearly three hours.

Ryan quickly discovered the men used their pay on the girls upstairs which filled in a lot of the income gap the clinic had been filling. This had the side effect of letting Ryan know the condition of the men as none of them had an STD since the bordello maintained the blood test requirement.

Jocey asked Ryan about having the men donate blood to replenish the clinic's blood bank. Ryan introduced her to Hanna and told him to deal with the request. He did not realize that by introducing the two, he laid the foundation for a romance as they connected immediately. Ryan learned of the romance when he came in at daylight one morning to find Hanna and Jocey leaving her room hand in hand. Neither spoke to him other than to say good morning as they passed him in the hallway.

Carol had moved back upstairs since there were paying clients in the building and Ciara told Ryan Carol may have found herself a steady man, and not just a client. Their own love making had moved to long, slow and loving which both found to be very enjoyable.

Ryan was relieved that Carol had returned upstairs and had found herself a man because as enjoyable as it was with her in bed with him and Ciara, he still felt the situation was not normal for him. In his past life he never considered a threesome as he thought of sex with his partner as a private experience. Was it being in a bordello that opened this up this part of his life or was there something else motivating him.

He was aware that Ciara had spent time with Jocey in her own room a few times while he was out on the street, but he never questioned her about such meetings since they had been lovers before he arrived on the scene. Still, things still did not feel right even though the people around him acted as if the world was normal for them. Maybe it was because he was from a different time in history.

Ryan would spend a lot of time up on the roof thinking, trying to rectify his actions with his feelings about those actions. As much as he felt he loved Ciara, he found having sex with Carol, even when Ciara was not involved came too easy for him, while sex with Margie was a strain. Was this part of his hibernation programming?

The Main Event

Ryan lay in Margie's bed, leaning back against the headboard reading the schedule for the Central Party meeting the upcoming week. It was complete with times and locations of parties and meetings outside of the main meeting of the Central Party and key members from Sacramento. He would have everyone under a single roof that needed to be removed to kick start the Revolution.

He had to move Margie's head from his crotch as she was playing with him, trying to get another rise out of him, so he could move off the bed. She grumbled as he moved her away and slid off the bed.

"Margie, this is certainly in depth. Are you certain each player will be at the locations at these times?"

"Yes, they'll be there, now come back to bed, please."

"That's a pleasant thought Margie, but I have to get back to camp and figure out how to get the men from Aspin to these locations without them being detected."

Ryan made that specific comment to see if Margie knew the men were already in the city.

"Maybe you can use trucks or buses? I'm sure you can figure it out in plenty of time. Please, come back to bed."

"Margie, you have expended thousands of dollars, maybe a couple of million setting this up, now is not the time to let your vagina distract you from your goal. What of the people left in Sacramento? How big a threat will they be?"

Margie just slumped on the bed and huffed before answering.

"No problem. I have people in place to control them if needed. The military, what there is of it, will not act without the

Party President issuing orders for them to move against you. He and everyone in the chain of command will be here, including the Military's Chief of Staff."

"Once we contain the Central Committee along with the President, who takes over?"

"You will Ryan, with me in the background, providing advice and support."

"Margie, I'm not qualified to lead a country. Good grief woman, is that the best you have?"

"Ryan, I just meant you lead the people to free elections and let them take over from there. Then you can do whatever you wish once that is accomplished."

"And the Secret Police? What of them?"

"They may be a problem, but with the Committee out of the way, they have no one to issue orders to them, just like the military."

"So, I stage a coup, and take over the government then, is that it?"

"Yes, basically that's it."

"I never considered this. I was hoping you had thought this through further than that. So, I take over the country with two hundred men. This will be one for the history books."

Ryan knew she had other plans in mind but was not telling him about them. She was using him for her own agenda and the people he was now responsible for. He knew that the Secret Police had been reformed within the city but it's effectiveness was limited because any new person was now suspect after he had basically wiped the old regime out. But how many of the new ones worked directly for Margie and what was their end purpose?

He got dressed as she grumbled while lying on the bed, exposing herself to him in hopes he would return for more. He just ignored her then gave her a quick kiss before leaving her mumbling about needing him some more tonight. Ryan knew what she was doing, she was trying to seduce him into doing whatever she asked of him, which meant whatever she had on her mind, directly affected what he was going to do. But he had other plans.

He drove back to the hotel but instead of going to his room and Ciara, he went to the roof to think. Ryan did something he rarely did as he removed the old photograph of Rhonda from his wallet and looked at it.

"Rhonda," He thought to himself, "It would have been better that the experiment had failed. But at the same time, I have gotten to know our Granddaughter. She is a good person stuck in a terrible situation and is making the most of her condition. I wish I had told you that I loved you, but I did not want to cause you any more pain knowing I would be gone from you if the experiment failed. I have found love with Ciara, even if I'm playing the male whore when away from her. I hate what I am doing in this life, but it is the cards I have been dealt, and I have to play them the best I can. Forgive me for any pain I caused you later in life. I do still have love for you in my heart."

Ryan sat for over an hour after he returned Rhonda's photo to his wallet. Margie was using him to set herself up as the key player once the Committee was eliminated, but how was still the question he had yet to get a handle on. How many of the Secret Police were in his company and what was their purpose once the coup took place? No one in his company had the Party Membership numbers tattooed on their shoulders, but that could also be part of the Secret Police's system. Margie had them, as did Linda, her daughter. Every female he had bedded from the Party had the tattoos, but none of his men.

He finally gave up and went to his room, showered and sat next to Ciara who was on the couch watching some stupid sitcom program about three girls and a guy living together, playing musical beds. In his time, this would be pure porn as the male actor took a female whenever he felt like it or the females wanted him to perform. Ciara commented that the hour-long program had to be filmed over several days as no man could go as long as the actor could or as many times within the hour program.

Her comment made him once more consider his own situation on how he was equipped and could perform longer and more often that he had been able to before going into hibernation. Then there was the women or young ladies he had been with since arriving. With very few excepts, those being the wives of Party members he had serviced, all of the females were physically in good shape. Maybe better shape than they should be for their lifestyle.

This was another piece of the puzzle that did not seem to fit properly in the universe. In several ways things seemed too perfect and too easy in a world on the brink of total destruction. He just held onto Ciara's hand and hoped this was real.

Ciara never commented on the fact he had gone to see Margie, as she just held his hand as they sat through the program. She took him to bed and just lay on his shoulder as they fell asleep with Ryan thinking he had to get her out of harm's way, along with Jocey before he moved on the Committee. But he had no idea how to accomplish that.

Two days before the Committee was to arrive in Denver, he had all of his people in the main hallway on the sixth floor, sitting down as best they could as he spoke to them.

"People, we are about to execute the plans given us by our sponsor, but I have a major problem in doing so. Although I do not know who you are, I know we have people in this company working directly for Misses Margie Davenport. People who are

134

either employees or members of the Secret Police working for her."

He let that sink in for a moment.

"Now I know my comment just cause a lot of suspicion amongst you people but let me say this. We are going to stage a coup against the Central Committee, one which is designed to return the power to the people. How blind does a person have to be to see the Party's programs have done nothing but destroy what was once the most powerful country on the planet? Why? For power. Power over others who have no choice in their lives and even if they are Party members, they have to march in lock step with the Party's program."

He paused.

"This country was founded on the principle of each person had the right to succeed or fail on their own abilities. I know what the history of this country truly is, and it is not the one currently taught to the children. I'm not going to give anyone a history lesson, but the power over this country is in the hands of people who never see the waste, never see the suffering of the people. I intend to show them that suffering. Look around you and open your eyes. The girls upstairs should not be having to sell their bodies to eat. The orphans below us should not have to rely on the girls upstairs selling themselves to provide them with food. The clinic should not have to rely on the girls whoring themselves out to provide medicines and care for the mass of homeless. If you think this is what this country should be, then you are part of the problem."

He expected someone to mention the fact he was living with one of the whores, but no one spoke up. He also knew that several of the men had all but moved in with a couple of the girls upstairs such as Carol. He then thought of stories from the Old West where lawmen often married prostitutes.

"Alright, I have said all I intend to say today. Captain Hanna, collect up the Lieutenants and we'll meet in my quarters in ten minutes. Dismissed."

Ryan left the door to his room open when he entered it knowing Ciara was in the clinic, working today. He took a big risk in speaking his mind, but it was a risk he was willing to take. He would meet with his officers unarmed. If one of them decided to kill him, so be it. He was tired of it all and wanted out. His only regret would as with Jacob, his son, he would not see or know the child growing in Ciara's womb.

His officers entered as a group, and just stood in the room waiting for him to speak as he looked out the windows at the city below him. He turned to the men almost expecting to feel a bullet enter his body.

"Gentlemen, the plan as it has been explained to me is that once we achieve the coup, I take over the government. Then we set up free elections to select a new government. First of all, I'm not qualified to be a head of any manner of government. Second, I seriously doubt what could be called free elections will happen. I have been told the military will not act against us, nor will the Secret Police. If that is so, the fix is in and this country will exchange one corrupt government for another. Pass the word that if what I suspect is true, then all of us, even the agents embedded with the rest of us are expendable. Nothing will save them except staying the course, protecting their teammates and hopefully we can pull this off."

"Major," Hanna spoke up. "Jocey has referred to you several times as her Grandfather, but you're not old enough."

Ryan told the officers about the hibernation program he had been involved with and how he came to be in Denver. He also told them about Margie having him brought to Denver to execute her plan which by itself never sounded right. He told them they could believe him if the wished or scoff at his story, but it was true as Jocey could verify.

He never told them his real name and Hanna only had Jocey's maiden name to connect him another identity. Ryan then put the question to the officers if they wished to complete the mission or disappear into the mass of homeless with a pocket full of money as he had also collected another packet of money from Margie to pay them.

"What do you figure our chances are?"   One of the Lieutenants asked him.

"Removing the Committee? One hundred percent. But I'll give no odds surviving the Revolution, unless we can guarantee the military and Secret Police does not make a move on us. We might have a bit of a problem with the local Police, but we'll just have to deal with them. One key is that according to the plan, we kill the Committee. If we kill them, then there is nothing stopping others from moving on us."

"So Major, the plan is to kill the Committee up front then hope to survive the coup?" The Lieutenant inquired.

"Yeah, I'd say that is a good assessment of the situation. Misses Davenport wants them all out of the way, which would give her an opening to take over, using me as her front man. The power behind the throne so to speak."

"And we are all expendable to her then?"

"That's how I see it even if she hasn't said so."

"That's not the briefing I received Major. But looking at it from your viewpoint, I'd say I was lied too. Major, I'm Secret Police out of Memphis. I was told I would be working to stem an internal coup and uprising by members of the Committee. Now that I've seen what I've seen here, I can no longer serve the

Committee. We've been told Denver is the show place for the Party and all I've seen is a waste, even worse than Memphis."

He paused.

"Major, if you will have me, trust me, I'm with you on this. And I'll identify myself to the men and tell them what I know, hopefully any other Secret Police will accept my thinking and move to safely side with us."

"Lieutenant, I have no choice but to trust you. My life is in your hands as yours is in the hands of the men under you. It's too late to weed out any dissenters, all we can do is hope for the best and pray we are successful."

"Major, what are you going to do about Misses Davenport?" Hanna asked.

"We have to let her play her hand, so we will know her final goal. After that is known, then we can make a decision on how to deal with her."

Ryan already knew what he was going to do with her, but he withheld that in case one of the men was able to warn her about the change in his plans. He picked up the bulging envelope with payroll stuff in it and tossed it to Hanna.

"Pay the men. There is a five-hundred-dollar bonus included in the envelope. See they get the money immediately and they have twenty-four hours before we make our first move."

Ryan waited until the officers had cleared the floor before he went down to see Ciara. As they were eating lunch, word came down from the bordello that every one of the girls were busy with the men dropping their entire pay at the appointment desk. Since each man had already cleared the blood tests and had not been out of the hotel, the girls were told to take an hour to clean up and wash themselves out before taking another client. Some of the men just dropped their pay on the desk, then left without taking advantage of the situation.

Ciara told Ryan that Prescott had a plan to get her and Jocey out of harm's way if things went wrong. Hanna came in a few minutes later with Jocey to eat and Ryan waved him over to sit with them.

"Jasper, find two clean teams, with no ties to Misses Davenport, if that is possible, and put them in street clothes. When we move out they will stay behind to protect Ciara and Jocey. If they have to bug-out of here, they are to go with them, protect them as well as possible."

"Grandfather...."

"Hush Jocey. You will do as I say in this matter. Talk to Prescott and take who you can with you. There is no way we can protect the hotel if things go sour, but hopefully some can be saved. The orphanage should be safe, but the bordello is another thing."

"Okay Grandfather, I'll get with Jim as soon as I finish lunch."

"Good. Jasper, to be fair, I would like you to stay back and oversee their safety, but that is favoring you over others. Sorry, but you will have to take part in the coup."

"Thanks for the consideration Major, but my place is watching your back. But there is one thing I would like to ask of you."

"Go ahead."

"If we survive this mess, would you allow me to marry your Granddaughter since her father is not available to ask for her hand."

139

"Grandfather, he knows about all I have done, and I've even taken two contracts since we got together. I've held nothing back from Jasper."

"If Jasper is okay with the situation, then who am I to say no. But Jocey, once you marry him, he will be your only lover. No more contracts."

"I've already told him that Grandfather. And thank you."

"Jasper, if she is anything like her Grandmother, then you are one lucky man. Now, let's finish our meals and find more pleasant things to discuss."

That evening Ryan was informed there were five men who identified themselves as either Secret Police or employees of Margie. All agreed with the Lieutenant and swore they would stand by Ryan in this endeavor. They did it publicly letting any other know they would not tolerate a traitor in this coup. Ryan was still concerned whether or not the quality of the oaths they made were valid. It all seemed too easy.

Ciara was passionate that night and again in the morning as they both knew he would be leaving early in the day. Reports had been coming in from the street people that the Committee had been arriving all through the night. There was a party scheduled tonight with all present, including Margie. Margie planned for the coup to take place at the Convention Center tomorrow when the Committee and associates formally met. This was not Ryan's plan.

The men slowly filtered out of the hotel using several exits while dressed as street people. Being the first part of fall and the temperature falling, this made it easy as the men could over dress for the movement, hiding their uniforms under over-sized coats. Their rifles were hidden in rolled up blankets like used to sleep under in an alley or a sidewalk. The men dirtied their faces to fit in as they moved to their staging areas to await Ryan's orders to move on the target.

The target location was the Embassy Suites Hotel next to the Convention Center as it was one of the few, real hotels left in Denver. It had been cleared of all guests for this meeting so only Party Committee members would be in the hotel, except for the few that lived in Denver such as Margie.

All of the players were accounted for and Ryan had an inside person who notified him when they were all in the Ball Room for the welcoming dinner and party. Ryan's orders for taking the ballroom was that the exterior security had to be taken out quickly and quietly and if possible, with minimum loss of life. This was also applied to the internal security if possible. No one except the prime movers and their aides would be in the ballroom according to the information provided by Margie.

Ryan went over the plan in his head one last time thinking Margie was going to get a shock when they took the ballroom. Every team had a mission. Some would secure the two bars where the personal bodyguards would most likely be waiting for their employers and other teams would secure the elevators and stairwells to prevent any guards from coming down to help once the word got out about the taking of the ball room.

He was taking three teams into the ball room while the rest would spread out to secure the hotel from intrusion. Timing was everything and he knew he had no control over that. Ryan gave the order to move.

In less than ten minutes the hotel was secured and time for him to make his entrance into the ballroom. Ryan was actually surprised how inept or lazy the security was around the most powerful people in the country and that worried him. Once more he was concerned he was being set up, but he knew for a fact Margie was in that room as he had witnessed her entering and no one had exited.

Every man was using silenced weapons but Ryan's M-4 was not so equipped. He entered a side door to the ballroom near the podium and let off a burst of fire into the ceiling as he moved to take center stage. As he did that, men moved into the ballroom and blocked the exits. People were yelling and screaming from his sudden, and very rude appearance. The people who were on the podium dropped to the floor as if to be out of the line of fire. Ryan went to the microphone at center stage.

"Quiet. I said quiet!"

The level of noise immediately dropped. He turned to the people on the podium stage.

"You people, get off the stage and with the rest of your kind. Move it before I lose my temper and patience."

He waited until the older members could be helped up and off the stage before he spoke again.

"You people have made a mess of this country and it's time for a change. The original plan was to kill all of you, every last one of you and change the system because you have caused so much suffering that you have ignored for power over the people of this country. Tonight, that changes."

He smiled at the crowd as he paused.

"Everyone strip, get nude right now or my men will remove your clothes for you."

He looked and found Margie standing with a surprised look on her face.

"Yes, I mean everyone."

He made a hand signal and one set of double doors opened with four, laundry carts being pushed inside.

"Once you have stripped, there is clothing in those carts for you to put on. Get dressed. You'll also find shoes for the ladies since where they are going, high-heels are not practical. Move it people, the longer you take, the higher your chances of not getting out of this room alive increases."

Ryan could see the hatred on Margie's face knowing he had double crossed her. She had planned not to be in the Central Committee meeting the next day claiming food poisoning when he was supposed to remove the Committee. She would ultimately take power and continue her father's dream of a socialists America. He had just destroyed that dream.

An hour later everyone in the ballroom had changed and were loaded into the box-bed trucks Margie had provided to transport the men and were headed towards the Aspin Camp. Once at the Aspin Camp, they would be guarded but without any manner of support, even the kitchen staff was gone. Half rations would be provided them, and since there was only one road to the camp, it would be guarded to prevent anyone attempting to walk the forty miles to find help, if they could find any at all.

Margie was able to get next to him before she was loaded onto a truck.

"You bastard, you could have had it all. The country, me, and more power than you ever imagined."

"I've always had the country, at least in my heart. One you can never live in or understand. I do not want power, only peace, yet your form of government gives no one peace, not even yourself as you plot to hold onto your power and gain more. As for having you, that's not saying much considering I'd have to constantly watch my back to keep you from putting a knife in it. Goodbye Margie."

Ryan suddenly felt tired and sat down in one of the hotel's lobby chairs as Hanna and the others took care of business. Phone calls were being made to the rooms where bodyguards were staying advising them of the situation and that they could leave, unarmed, without a problem.

143

He sat in the chair thinking that Rhonda would be proud of what he had done by not killing the Party Leaders, then he thought about Ciara, and where they might go to get away for all of this. Something still did not feel right in his mind, but suddenly, he was too tired to consider what that might be.

The darkness of sleep overtook Ryan as if someone had thrown a switch, turning him off.

Assessment

She looked at the monitor with the animation frozen on the screen and the mental dialogue frozen at the bottom. A tear flowed down her cheek as she accepted the words with love.

Rhonda Petersen turned to Doctor Browning and smiled. What Ryan/Bryon had experienced for over a year, they viewed in less than eight hours. She looked through the observation window at the frosted chamber which held Ryan/Bryon and smiled. On the floor behind her playing with Nerf Blocks was their son, Jacob.

"I wasn't wrong about him was I Doctor Browning?"

"No Rhonda, you were not wrong. I would say this also proves he did not murder those people he was condemned to die for, but since the execution has been sealed there is no way we can petition to have him pardoned for that. But as Bryon Peterson, he will be free to live however he wants after we get him thawed out and back in condition."

"Will he remember Ciara?"

"Rhonda, most likely he will, but we will not know until he is out and can be counseled. But as you have seen, he never forgot you."

"Yes, he never forgot me. Who came up with this program? The animation was so lifelike, at times you thought you were looking are real people, not animation. And the story line, where did it come from?"

"Gamers came up with the program. It's the first, truly interactive program and very expensive. The story came from one of our staff, an amateur writer who has a couple electronic books out. I have to say, every time Bryon felt something was missing, it was because it was left out of the script for him to put in if possible."

"I noticed a few times we did not see him in action so to speak, such as when he took Carol to Ciara's room. Or during his planning of the Revolution. Was that just part of the program?"

"We're not sure what caused that. Every action he took should have been up on the screen, but it wasn't. It was almost as if he was controlling the program, prohibiting us from seeing parts of it. That's another thing the programmers are going to have to investigate."

"Thank you for letting me sit in on this."

"Not a problem, Rhonda. The work you did getting him here played a major part in making this experiment work, and of course the work in setting this program up more than gave you the right to see what he really was thinking."

"It was odd watching him make love to those women. I mean what we were seeing was anime, but it was still active in his mind. It was as real to him as if he was not in that chamber. I wonder what another man would have done in those situations?"

"We have two others in hibernation now, and before we wake them up, we'll run them through the same program and see how they react. But what we were seeing was part of his basic personality, his nature if you will. In his mind he hated what he was doing but moved on through it as if fated to do so. The recording of his actions will be reviewed over and over again by other shrinks to determine if he was acting on emotion or just accepted his fate and moved on. But I have to agree with you that at first, he just accepted his fate, but as it wore on his conscious, he adjusted as best he could and moved on."

"Doctor Browning, there is a lot missing from the script, bits and pieces he filled in without showing his hand even to the anime. How is that possible?"

"That's something we do not know. Our programmers will take the program apart bit by bit and maybe they'll find the answers. But they only laid in the base program and it adapted to his actions. Everything he did is him, not the program."

Awakening

Bryon slowly woke to dim light in trying to peel his eyelids back and a throbbing in his head. His throat felt like the Iraqi desert from breathing the dried, purified air inside the capsule. He sensed more than observed the capsule top being removed as he could only lay still, thinking he had made the journey and survived.

"Bryon, can you hear me?" A muffled voice spoke from his right.

Bryon tried to speak but could not voice an answer.

"That's alright Bryon, we'll get you something to drink in a minute, but just lie still as we get you all disconnected."

Lying still was easy for Bryon as he felt as weak as a baby. Removing the IV's was no problem, but the removal of the catheter was almost painful since it had been in so long. All the wires connected to sensors placed on his body were disconnected then a cool, damp rag was placed over his eyes. He felt a straw touch his lips and opened his mouth enough to accept it, and then sucked on it the best he could. The water was cool and tasted a bit metallic as it soothed the dryness in his throat.

"Bryon, we are going to put some clinical shorts on you then set you up. Do not try to help us, just let it happen." The voice spoke again.

The damp rag over his eyes seemed to help as did the cool water eased the dryness of his throat. He had no idea how many people were in the room helping him and at that moment he did not care. He passed the test and all he wanted now was out of it.

Soon they had the shorts on him, then sitting upright with his legs off the capsule base. One person was holding him up from behind then two sets of hands lifted him off the base and into what he figured was a wheelchair. Straps were placed over his chest to hold him upright then someone removed the rag and began to carefully wipe his eyelids with a soft, damp cloth.

"Bryon try to open your eyes, but do not be alarmed if you have trouble focusing at first."

Bryon carefully opened his eyes, blinking rapidly as the dim light bothered them. The optic nerves had not been used in so long they were slow to react and adjust to the light. Slowly the blurs before him became figures then he was finally able to see the doctor standing in from of him in scrubs and wearing a surgical mask.

"Bryon, how do you feel?"

"Weak. I take it the experiment is a success?" Bryon's voice was weak as he spoke.

"Yes, it was a grand success. You've been out sixty-one months. It's taken nearly a full month to safely revive you."

"Great. Tell me, what shape is the country in?"

"Better than you left it. New president who isn't taking crap from anyone and putting people back to work."

"So, no nuclear war?"

"No Bryon, in fact the President for the most part stopped one. Soon after he took office, told the world that he had signed orders to all of the military field commanders that if anyone attacks the Continental United States and destroys the Command and Control from Washington, they are to act on their own and retaliate accordingly. This had the effect of some of the major players to step hard on the small players who just might try such a thing."

"That's good to hear. Doc, I feel like I had the weirdest dream. Is it possible to dream under those conditions?"

"Let's get you cleaned up and in a regular bed, then we can discuss what has happened while you were asleep after you've had a chance to recover."

"Alright. Is there any way I can contact Rhonda? I have something I have to tell her."

"She's here in the complex. Let's give you a day to recover before we allow you any visitors."

"Sure, you're the Doctor."

He was taken to a room where he was carefully washed, then another room where he was placed, sitting up in a bed. A nurse wearing a facemask was there to assist him in all manner of things. She held a glass of warm liquid which had a ginger taste that he sipped on through a straw. She told him it was a nutrient drink to help replenish vitamins and minerals he had lost during hibernation.

A barber came in and cut his hair and trimmed the beard that had grown while in hibernation. When Bryon ask why he had not shaved the beard off, the barber told him a lady asked for the beard to be left neatly trimmed. Bryon laughed knowing who had made that request.

It was late in the afternoon of the second day that he looked up to see Rhonda standing in the door with a child on her hip. He started crying which caused her to cry as she moved to the side of the bed, leaned over and kissed him. Bryon was weak, but he was able to raise his hand up and touched her face.

"Rhonda, I never told you I loved you. I'm so sorry I never did."

"Hush Bryon, I knew you loved me even if you never said the words. And this is your son, Jacob."

"Hi Jacob." Bryon spoke to his son.

"Mommy, is this Dada?"

"Yes, Jacob, he's been asleep for a long time, but he is awake now."

Jacob leaned over to the point that Rhonda had to let him down on Bryon's lap. He looked at Bryon for a long time before reaching up and hugged his neck. Bryon hugged him back and was sobbing as he placed a kiss on Jacob's cheek.

"Why are you crying Dada?"

"I'm crying because I am so happy to see you and your mother. I'm so happy that you are not a dream."

Rhonda and Jacob spent an hour visiting with Bryon, bringing him up to date about how her life had been while waiting for him to complete the experiment. Bryon asked her to marry him even though there was paperwork saying they were already married. She accepted his proposal but told him they would wait until he could consummate their wedding. He told her he could wait if she could.

After Rhonda and Jacob left, Doctor Browning came to visit along with a Phycologists to examine him. When Bryon brought up the dream, he was told that it was not a dream, but an inter-active computer program which he was a part of. The game responded to his thoughts and actions. Bryon sat quiet for a long time before asking several questions.

"Was it my idea to make my Granddaughter a prostitute?"

"You remember that?"

"Doctor, I remember everything about it. Was it my idea?"

"No, that part was just to see your reaction, but once you basically accepted her condition based upon the situational scenario, the game adjusted itself and built the bordello within the clinic. From that point on, the game kept testing you to see your reactions."

"How did I do? From your standpoint?"

"Better than we considered once the program basically went off the deep end. We came close to terminating the program but your actions within it told us to keep you moving in it. We could see your thoughts as you pondered your situation and even though you disliked the position you were placed in, you tried to adapt, and utilize what you had to survive. It was also your concern for the females in the bordello and the orphans that surprised us."

"Surprised you how?"

The Phycologist blushed.

"Before you reached that stage, I predicted you would work your way through the bordello never considering that you would hook up with Ciara and basically ignore the other girls. We introduced the idea of Ciara having you take Carol to bed just to get your reaction."

"Doctor, somewhere in my mind I knew things were not natural. I just went with the flow most of the time. Hell Doc, whoever designed the females in the program did a damn good job. Even now to me, they were as real as you sitting there right now."

"Bryon, to be honest, all of the females in the program were built from screen captures of actresses who did nude parts, female athletes, and models with the programmer playing with their looks based on information we had from Rhonda's notes and interviews concerning you. The computer programmer changed bits and pieces such as hair color and length, to shape of faces so you would not recognize any of them in case you had seen the movies. And we read your thoughts about your own enhancement, which was done by the programmer, just to see how you'd react. The rest was all in your head."

152

"The programmer watches too much porn then. Now am I at risk of having a flashback or such considering what I did outside of the hotel?"

"Only time will tell Bryon, but the fact you now know it was never real should give you relief from nightmares or flashbacks so to speak."

"One other thing. Rhonda's voice on the recordings I saw of her in the video, and Jacob? Were they part of this?"

"Rhonda returned as she promised when she knew it was getting close to your awakening. We briefed her on our plans, so she recorded her part bringing Jacob in before we initiated the test program. One of our male interns stood in for Jacob in the later recordings, and make-up helped age Rhonda. This was where we developed Jocey and her part in it. Rhonda actually predicted much of what you did in the test program based upon knowing about her and Jacob."

"Thanks Doc. One other thing that I would like to understand."

"What's that Bryon?"

"Ciara. She was so different from the Tiara character, more like Rhonda except for the skin tone and Asian looks, of course, but body and personality once past the sexual side of things seemed so much like Rhonda."

"Bryon, that was Rhonda, as best as we could get her. We already had a lot of data on her from before the experiment, before she met you. The programmers had a very in-depth questionnaire which she filled out and they plugged that information into the program and into Ciara's character. We had to adjust it from time to time such as dealing with Carol, but otherwise, Ciara was Rhonda."

"So that's why I fell in love with her so quickly, so easily. Thanks again Doc."

The first time Rhonda came to visit him without Jacob, he asked her about Ciara's aggressiveness during sex considering she was supposed to have been patterned after her based upon the questionnaire Rhonda had filled out. Rhonda blushed as she told him that was closer to true than she had exhibited when they were together.

"Bryon, before I married Stephen, I had an interesting sex life. I experimented in college and had a female lover for nearly two years. He knew about my life but never asked for more than I could give him one on one, and I've not taken a female lover since. As tempting as it was to get crazy with you in bed, I held back because I didn't want to scare you away, especially when I discovered I was in love with you."

"Anyway, when they gave me the questionnaire, and explained the scenario for the test program, I answered as honestly as I could, kept the answers as honest as possible, exposing myself to everyone, including you. I took a risk in scaring you away, but if you were in better shape, I'd show you just how much like Ciara I really am."

Bryon reached out and took her hand and held it for a minute before responding.

"Rhonda, from what I remember of that program and of Ciara, it will only be you and me, no others, but you can be yourself in our bed remembering that the man in the program was enhanced, while I'm just a normal man."

Rhonda lightly laughed.

"Bryon, you are more than enough man for me as you are. If you were in better condition, I'd show you how much right now even though I suspect there are cameras watching us in this room."

Bryon laughed.

"Honey, I suspect we are going to spend a lot of time exhausted. I love you Baby."

"I love you too Bryon."

Starting Over

A month after he was removed from the chamber, quarters were made available for him and Rhonda with a separate room for Jacob, so they would have privacy. They were married two days later in a civil ceremony, with Jacob standing between them. It took four months of physical therapy and exercise, along with a solid diet before Bryon was released from the experiment.

The lawyer, Jameson, visited with him before his release to transfer the title to his old property and that of his mothers to him. The people he worked for had bought it at auction and held it for him if he still wanted it. He accepted the deeds along with a bank account that would keep him comfortable the rest of his life.

Jameson also told him the people who had framed him were no longer a threat to the country as they had over played their hand and were identified, and then dealt with. Jameson never commented further on how they were dealt with other than the smile on his face.

Bryon had a new house built where his old house had once stood and put a few head of cattle on the property and became a gentleman rancher.

Jacob was seven when Rhonda announced she was once again expecting. She gave birth to another son who she named Ryan which got a laugh from Bryon.

Bryon wrote a fictional book using the dream as the background telling the story as it happened while cleaning up the sex part as best he could with Rhonda's help. Just as it was being published, Rhonda gave Bryon a surprise in that she was pregnant again.

His book went on to become a best seller in Science Fiction and Rhonda gave Bryon a little girl whom they named Ciara.

The Final Report

During Bryon's recuperation period, he was interviewed daily by the doctor's, scientists, and even the computer programmers concerning his time in hibernation.

During the early stages of Hibernation, they had in fact fed him the equivalence of a college education in History and Physics. He was given a six-hour written exam based on the courses he was fed, and the final results were that he completed the exam and was awarded a Bachelor's Degree in History, with a Minor in Physics from the University of Utah.

It was during the final six months of his hibernation that he was given the memories and electronic Ranger training to determine if he could be so conditioned. The animation program proved he had retained the memories and knowledge given him and it was proved that those memories could be adjusted during the test program. The adjustments were dealt with during Ciara's probing of his mind.

One determination was made that Bryon's innate personality make-up was never over-written by the data implanted during hibernation and was constantly attempting to break though the conditioning thus giving him the mental sensation that something was not right with the situation he was in during the animation test program.

It was noted that Hypnotists claimed that even though they could get their subjects to do some things, they could not make a person act against their innate personality, make them do something which goes against their core beliefs.

The final determination in the case of Bryon Petersen was that with careful planning and programming, adjustments and training within the perimeters of a person's personality could be accomplished without stress on the subject. Future subjects would be judged against Bryon, using him as the benchmark as the programs were refined and enhanced.

Bryon was interviewed and tested five years later on retention of knowledge and passed with high marks. After thirty years of experimentation and research, they had a proven concept for sending a hundred people on a mission to Mars and beyond. Bryon would live to see the first of many missions to Mars and further out into space. But no one would know of his part in preparing for such journeys, which pleased him as he did not want the publicity.

About The Author

Leon Michaels is the author of several novels and short stories that reflect his twenty-three years of military service.   Michaels enlisted in the Marine Corps in 1970 and has memberships in the Veterans of Foreign Wars, the American Legion, the Disabled American Veterans organizations, NRA, and Rotary International.   In 1971, he married his high school sweetheart, raised three daughters and has three grandsons. He calls Creek County, Oklahoma home.

83130035R00095

Made in the USA
Lexington, KY
11 March 2018